Crazy Man Michael

Also by Jim Lusby

MAKING THE CUT
FLASHBACK
KNEELING AT THE ALTAR

CRAZY MAN MICHAEL
Jim Lusby

VICTOR GOLLANCZ
LONDON

Copyright © Jim Lusby 2000

The right of Jim Lusby to be identified as the author
of this work has been asserted by him in accordance with
the Copyright, Designs and Patents Act, 1988.

First published in Great Britain in 2000
by Victor Gollancz
An imprint of Orion Books Ltd
Orion House, 5 Upper St Martin's Lane,
London WC2H 9EA

A CIP catalogue record for this book
is available from the British Library

Typeset by SetSystems Ltd, Saffron Walden
Printed and bound in Great Britain by
Clays Ltd, St Ives plc

To Pearse, for a strange affair . . .

one

Wearing only a sleeveless blue slip, she was sitting at her dressing table, grooming her hair with a lavender brush. She had long, gleaming black hair and she was stroking it with a slow, insistent rhythm, the movement keeping her muscles tight and rippling along her naked shoulders, and her posture – with both her arms raised and working behind her head – exaggerating the attractions of her figure . . . until the brush's teeth suddenly snagged on a knot by the roots and she swore quietly. She reached out then to switch on a shaded lamp and worked for a while with her fingers, disentangling the problem with the hair.

When she was finished, she put the brush beside the lamp on her dressing table. A little sweat from her palm glistened on the handle under the light. She pulled a paper handkerchief from a box and dried her hands, dropping the crumpled tissue into a wicker basket by her feet afterwards. Then she glanced sharply upwards into the mirror again, her bright eyes flashing for an instant in her shadowy face.

It was a pose of hers McCadden was already too familiar with. That sideways glance across the naked shoulder, against the movement of her body. A quarter of a century before, when McCadden was in his early teens, she'd overused it in publicity stills.

In the dull light from the bedroom lamp, it was possible to believe that those twenty-five years had taken nothing away from her. And perhaps that was the illusion she craved. Youth. Fame. The lost attractions of her own past.

McCadden coughed lightly. Standing by the foot of her unmade bed, he smoothed the rug that was under his shoes, straightening the rucks he'd made when he'd stumbled over it a minute earlier. He said, 'Your front door was open. I knocked a couple of times before stepping in, but there was no answer.'

She nodded slightly at his reflection in the dressing-table mirror 'Yes, I know.'

'Are you Eleanor Shiels?'

'Uh-huh.'

'You didn't answer when I called your name.'

'Yes, I know.'

Limited vocabulary. Narrow range of responses.

McCadden offered a smile. 'I'm sorry if I startled you.'

'You didn't.'

'My name's McCadden, Ms Shiels. Carl McCadden. I'm a Garda inspector.'

'Uh-huh.'

'Could I talk to you for a while? I can wait for you in the room outside.'

'Make yourself at home.'

'And the light switch . . . ?'

'It's on the wall inside the door. On your right.'

The cottage was small. The outside room, leading to a cramped scullery and tiny bathroom, was even narrower than the bedroom. Lighting it, from a soft, blue-tinted bulb, McCadden glanced at the furniture he'd groped a path through in darkness a few minutes earlier. Most of it was in plain wood, rough and serviceable, and possibly handcrafted by some local carpenter.

He scanned the fittings and the ornaments, looking for insights into the owner. There were no musical instruments, he noticed. And there were no records. No vinyl. No CDs. No cassette tapes. The white walls held a few standard Dali prints, a rough African mask and a thin watercolour of the headland they were on; but there were no photographs from Eleanor Shiels's career, no posters advertising her gigs, no artwork from her record sleeves. Nothing at all to suggest that she was once hailed, in the trade magazines, as the voice of the new Ireland.

2

One of the *earlier* new Irelands. Back in the mid-seventies.

In the opposite corner of the room, there was a squat writing desk. Its surface held a ream of typing paper, a few current affairs magazines and a stack of colour photographs. McCadden walked across to look at the top print. Surprised, he used his index finger to slide it off the pile and reveal the next, quickly repeated the movement and went on sifting through the batch in the same style until he'd reached the end.

The photographs were recent and used the interior of the cottage as a setting. The desk itself appeared in the background of some of them and on the desk there was a national newspaper with the date quite clearly visible. 26 July. Less than three weeks ago.

Shot on expensive equipment, perhaps by a good professional or a gifted amateur, the prints offered slight variations on a single theme. Eleanor Shiels featured in all of them. Mostly, she was naked. Occasionally, something flimsy was loosely draped over parts of her body. Domestic items. Like a net curtain, for instance. A small pillowcase. The corner of a blanket. She was bound in all of them. But tastefully. Or *considerately*, maybe. With kitchen towels. Bed sheets. Cotton belts. All soft materials. There were no chains. No handcuffs. No metals at all. The lighting and the focus were also soft. And so were the poses. One even used that famous glance across the naked shoulders, against the movement of her body; but whether as pastiche or homage, with irony or nostalgia, it was impossible to tell.

McCadden was sitting in the harder of the two armchairs in front of the open fireplace, after replacing the prints and moving away from the writing desk, when Eleanor Shiels finally joined him from the bedroom. She'd pulled on black denim jeans and a loose black sweater. She still looked stunning, as mysterious as a cat burglar in her dark outfit, but the stronger light also showed the lines on her face, the slight heaviness around her waist and hips that came with the mid-forties. And she was wary. The caution holding back any expression from her features, leaving her seeming bland, devoid of mood or personality.

McCadden gestured his apologies. 'You must've been getting ready for bed . . . '

3

She sat in the other armchair, flicked imaginary dust from her thighs. 'It doesn't matter.'

'Do you always leave your front door open at night?'

'Isn't it the custom in the country?'

'Not any more, I don't think.'

She shrugged. 'Maybe I'm out of touch.'

'And not at night, anyway. Only during the day. As I remember.'

'Is there some danger?'

'Well, the standard advice is to be more aware of personal security—'

'Some *specific* danger. Here on the headland.'

'No, nothing like that.'

'Then why worry?'

McCadden looked at her for a moment, his eyebrows slightly raised. He said, 'Ms Shiels, three months ago you reported to the local station that some person or persons unknown seemed to be watching this cottage.'

'I was mistaken.'

'Hopefully.'

'There was nothing to worry about.'

'Which is always good to hear.'

'Is that what you've come about?'

He thought about it, reluctant to let the angle fade so quickly, but finally shook his head. 'No.'

'What, then?'

'I'm looking for someone. A man named Tony Wallace.'

She'd already slipped past impatience. Now she was irritated. When she answered, her tone was sharper, almost wearily dismissive. '*Who?*'

'Tony Wallace. Also known as Rookie Wallace.'

'*Rookie* Wallace? Good God!'

'The name doesn't mean anything to you?'

'Does it *seem* as if it does?'

'We're encouraged not to rely on impressions.'

'I'm not familiar with the name. I don't know anyone named Tony Wallace.'

'He might be using another.'

'Of course.'

'He's a middle-aged man. About forty years old. Six foot. Dark hair and complexion. Probably unshaven. Rough-looking guy. He's got a scar running horizontally across his left cheek. He was grazed by a bullet a few years ago. I'm sure you'd recognize him if you came across him.'

'No doubt.'

'He's a stranger, not from this area.'

'Are you questioning everyone on the headland?'

'You're the first.'

'Why? Just the luck of the draw?'

'No. He claims he knows you.'

'*Claims?*' she repeated. She sighed heavily, as if crushed by his stupidity. 'How well have you done your homework, Inspector?' she wondered.

'I know about your career, Ms Shiels,' McCadden assured her. 'I accept that fame can act as a lure to the most unstable of characters, feeding their fantasies.'

'Then you'll understand my scepticism.'

'But that's not the case with Wallace.'

She sighed and shook her head 'I've never seen the man you described, Inspector. I can't help you.'

She gestured her regrets and stood up, waiting for him to follow, but McCadden sat on, contemplating the brick wall she offered and wondering if chipping at it was going to be worth his while. He sensed that she was hiding something. People's reluctance to pursue the details always made him suspicious. People's suppression of their natural curiosity, their fears, their self-interest. She hadn't asked, for instance, if Wallace was dangerous. She hadn't wondered if he was a criminal, if he'd smashed his way out of prison or tricked his way out of a psychiatric hospital. She hadn't established if he'd made any threats against her.

Maybe she already knew the answers. Maybe she didn't really care.

When he finally stood, McCadden offered his hand. Eleanor

Shiels accepted. But her touch was light. And very, very brief. As he headed for the front door, he expected to drag her along in his wake. She stayed where she was, staring after him.

Opening the door, he turned and said, 'I suppose you'll remember my name. If you need to contact me.'

She didn't commit herself. Just smiled faintly.

He added, 'I'll probably take a quick look around. You don't mind, do you?'

This time, he didn't expect a response. And didn't get any.

two

Outside, the wind had lifted again. Mid-August, but the weather not keeping pace with the calendar. Not here, anyway. Fifty metres from where McCadden stood, the south Atlantic swelled and broke against the jagged rocks of the exposed headland. A treacherous place for shipping. It always had been. For a thousand years the seabed below had collected wrecks, coveting everything from Viking longboats to modern trawlers.

McCadden drew in the damp night air and looked around, his eyes adjusting again to the darkness. The cottage, rebuilt from the ruins of an older dwelling abandoned in harsher times, was the last on the headland. Another renovated cottage stood about thirty metres away. Further back, where the road ended and turned into the pot-holed track that challenged a car's suspension, there was a cluster of modern bungalows. And on the other side of the bay, across almost five kilometres of surging water, there were the holiday lights of Tramore, from where the faint sounds of carnival music and human shrieking were occasionally carried on the wind.

McCadden used a small torch to illuminate the immediate area. Not knowing what he was looking for. And not finding anything at first.

There was a narrow gap between the walls of the building and the hedge of blackberry bushes that almost completely surrounded it. But the space held no surprises. None of the cottage's windows had been forced or damaged. The earth, still soft from the rains of the last few days, was undisturbed.

He walked around the hedge, beyond a barbed-wire fence and into a stony, uneven field that a local farmer obviously used for grazing his cattle. And nothing there but the imprint of hooves. And cow dung. And deep impressions of tractor wheels.

He was turning away, already weary with working in the country, when the sweeping beam from his torch caught a piece of flapping white material that had been snagged on the wire. It might've been the remains of a plastic shopping bag. It might've been a strip from the farmer's Sunday shirt, he joked to himself. He couldn't tell. But even as he moved towards it, he lost interest in it again. It turned out not to be significant in itself, but only as a pointer. Because beyond it, between the wire and the hedge, a little clearing had been trampled down by human feet.

McCadden parted the strands of wire, twisted the barbs around each other to hold them in place and stooped to climb through the gap. When he stood upright again, he could see above the hedge. In fact, he had a clear view of Eleanor Shiels's bedroom window. And provided he didn't move, didn't drift into the overspill of light from the window, he was obviously obscured himself.

But the last occupant had also taken chances.

The evidence suggested that a cigarette smoker had watched from this spot on separate occasions. Definitely twice. Probably more. At McCadden's feet, there were several crushed cigarette butts. Not filters, as he discovered when he crouched to examine them. And not machine produced. Ones that were rolled by the smoker, using filter papers, loose tobacco, small pieces of cardboard as home-made holders. The way a joint was usually rolled. Some of them had been trodden into the ground, leaving only a corner or a curve still visible. Others were still on the surface, sodden from the recent rain and on the point of disintegration. But all of them had been burned by someone so addicted to the weed that they were willing to risk exposing their position to keep puffing.

McCadden took a plastic Ziploc bag from a pocket of his leather jacket, gathered the butts and sealed the bag after dropping them in. The harvesting had taken him sideways.

When he stood again, a bramble grazed his right cheek and the shoulder of his jacket caught on a thorn. His reaction made him jerk. The movement almost pulled the snared jacket off his shoulder. Cursing, he eased back, his left hand working to free his clothes without tearing the material.

He didn't hear anyone approaching. Had no idea he'd attracted company.

From behind, a flash of light suddenly hit his profile, blinding him for a moment. He thought at first it was the flashbulb of a camera, recording his entanglement on film. Thought it was a joke. Maybe Eleanor Shiels, ironically referring to the photographs of her he'd peeped at earlier.

But the light returned quickly and then held steady. And a man's voice shouted at him aggressively, 'Stay where you are, you!'

Shielding his eyes, McCadden called back quietly, 'It's all right, I'm—'

'I'll tell you what you are!' the voice cut him off.

It wasn't a local accent. A countryman's, but with the flavour of the west rather than the south coast about it. Kerry? Clare? Stuck with his back to it, dazzled by the glare if he tried to turn, McCadden felt vulnerable, irritated, a little worried.

'I'm a garda!' he said sharply. 'Do you understand? Put the light down!'

There was no response. In the silence the sound of an electric organ drifted on the wind from the neighbour's cottage nearby. It swelled for an instant. And then died away again. Before McCadden could recognize the tune.

'Did you hear me?' he called.

'I heard you, all right,' the voice confirmed. Sceptical now. Disparaging. 'You'll have identification so, will you?'

McCadden retrieved his ID with his left hand and flipped the wallet open into the light above his head. The torch faltered for a second before being switched off.

'I'm sorry, sir. I didn't recognize you. I, ah . . . '

McCadden turned, but still couldn't distinguish anything. A bulky shadow loomed in front of him, about five metres away. 'Who are you?'

'Sergeant Mullaney, sir. From Dunmore East.'

Funny how knowledge informed the eyes. Now the peaked cap and heavy greatcoat of the guard's uniform were visible. Polished buttons even glistened in the moonlight.

McCadden stepped back through the gap he'd made in the fence, laughing easily about the encounter. 'You couldn't be from Dunmore,' he joked. It was a fishing harbour, a couple of kilometres to the east along the coast. 'Not with an accent like that.'

'*Stationed* in Dunmore, sir.'

'I see. Right.'

'I was actually born in Lisdoonvarna. I'm a Clareman.'

'Lisdoonvarna. The Mecca of Irish bachelors.'

'So they say, sir. I'm actually married myself, you see, so—'

'Is this on your usual beat?' McCadden slipped in. 'Brownstown Head, here.'

The sergeant stumbled, laughed uneasily. 'No, ah . . . No. It's just with the report and all.'

'What report?'

'The woman lives there, she reported prowlers might be around.'

'Wasn't that some months ago?'

'It was, yes, that's right. But she was once famous, you see. So they say, anyway. That sort of thing attracts a queer kind . . . Sometimes I drop down to see if things are all right.'

'Seen anyone prowling?'

'Not so far, no. But you never . . . know.'

McCadden grunted, then loudly slapped the pockets of his jacket. 'You wouldn't have a cigarette, would you?' he wondered.

Anxious to please, the sergeant eagerly hiked a corner of his greatcoat and rummaged in a trouser pocket. The packet he offered was of a popular brand of filter-tipped.

McCadden grimaced. 'Anything stronger than that?'

The sergeant was suddenly embarrassed, worrying about his image, his virility. 'I used to *eat* the damn things, sir, to tell you the truth, you know, but . . . They say the low-tar lads reduce the old risk of doing damage to the lungs . . . '

As McCadden listened to a rural spin on the industry spiel,

Eleanor Shiels started moving again behind the window of her bedroom. Caught between the lamp on her dressing table and the thin curtains, she offered a sharply focused shadow when she stopped and stood still again. She was in profile. And she seemed to be naked. Raising her hands behind her head, she twisted her long black hair into a tight bun that she then clipped to keep secure.

The sergeant went on talking, but his eyes drifted away from McCadden and his head slowly swivelled. A tall man, over six and a half feet, he still had to strain to look fully over the hedge from where he stood, stretching painfully on his toes. But it wasn't the physical effort that showed on his rough country features. It was a look of raw lust. And it was so consuming that he was unaware he was a spectacle himself.

McCadden glanced away, not wanting to draw attention to his own observations. He gestured towards the neighbouring cottage, from where the sound of organ music, playing something recognizable now, was blowing across again. 'Who lives over there?'

The sergeant started. He swivelled guiltily, but found that he wasn't being stared at. 'What?'

'Over there?'

The sergeant followed the direction of McCadden's nod, his expression jerking from furtiveness through confusion to disgust. 'Oh! Some odd fellow came down here from Dublin, sir. Newburn, I think his name is.'

'Odd?'

'Vegetarian, they say.'

'How long has he lived here?'

'Years, now.'

'Right. Have you seen anyone new around the area lately?'

The sergeant risked a laugh, swelling back now into his natural boorishness. 'Dunmore's a holiday village, sir. Nearly everyone you meet is a stranger this time of year.'

'I meant, residents.'

'There's the pharmaceutical factory. Lisenter. They got in a few new executives from outside the last few months.'

'Bit too dressy for what I'm looking for. Ever notice a big guy with a scar across his left cheek? Rough looking. The kind of character you'd pull over just to check on.'

'Can't say I have, sir, no.'

'Right,' McCadden sighed again. 'Maybe I'll wander over and have a chat with the neighbour. Newburn, did you say?'

'Sonny Newburn, sir. He works at the ESB office in Waterford.'

'Which way did you come in?'

'What?'

'You'd better lead. You seem more familiar with the ground.'

But the sergeant was reluctant to leave. Furtively he sneaked a last, disappointed look over the hedge, craning again just as the light was switched off in Eleanor Shiels's bedroom.

'That torch of yours still working?' McCadden encouraged him.

'I suppose, yes . . .'

The sergeant led them towards the neighbouring cottage, then turned left along a rutted path and came out by an iron gate at the entrance to the field, where McCadden had parked earlier. Mullaney had pulled up tight behind the Mondeo. But not in a squad car, McCadden noticed. In his own private Astra.

Was Mullaney coming off duty? Just clocking in? Taking much of a detour?

'What's it like?' McCadden wondered innocently.

'What, sir?'

'Living in Dunmore. I suppose it's smaller than your home town. Do you live in the village itself?'

But the sergeant's liveliness had faded. Frustrated in the purpose of his journey, he was eager to get away now. Small talk had no further attraction.

'It's not too bad, sir,' he confirmed curtly. 'Not too bad. Will you, ah, be wanting me to go in with you? To Newburn.'

McCadden shook his head. 'No. Thanks.'

'Well, ah . . . goodnight, then, sir.'

'Night, Sergeant.'

McCadden stood by the boot of his own Mondeo, watching the sergeant fumbling with the car keys, hunching his big frame into the slightly cramped cabin of the Astra and painfully manoeuvring back and forth across the pot-holes in the lane, until the car was facing again towards the road.

An uncomfortable man, he thought.

three

Sonny Newburn didn't smoke.

He didn't drink, either. He wore an old-fashioned cardigan under a dull brown suit, didn't invite any intimacies and hid behind a regime of lifeless habits.

He looked like a disappointed man. On the walls of the living room in his cottage there were a couple of graduation certs from an English music academy, dating back to the late fifties. Maybe he'd once imagined something more accomplished than being a clerical officer with the Electricity Supply Board, somewhere more exotic than Brownstown Head to enliven his retirement. And maybe living beside a musical legend who'd thrown it all away was a little cruel for him.

His failure showed. Every question was taken on the defensive. Every answer cautiously measured.

A small, nervous man, he shut off the recording he was listening to when McCadden knocked, put in a long time agonizing over his next move and only opened the door after McCadden held his ID to the lens of the spyhole in the wood.

'Mr Newburn?' McCadden asked through the narrow gap.

Newburn blinked, weighing the purpose of the query, the consequences of a response. 'Yes?'

'Inspector McCadden, from Waterford. There have been reports of a prowler in the area recently. Would you mind if I asked you a few questions?'

'What kind of questions?'

'Could I step in for a while?'

The cottage was stuffy. Not too *warm*, even though the central heating was on, but airless and stale, smelling of cheap sprays and withered flowers, old books and discarded clothes. The past accumulated everywhere, cluttering the room. On the wooden floor, unsteady piles of dried old newspapers shifted precariously whenever there was movement around them. Yellowing documents, tied together with elastic bands or held in frayed folders, covered the surfaces of chairs and tables. A glass cabinet in the corner held stacked videotapes of outdated television shows, which twenty years earlier had nostalgically explored a bygone age. All uselessly preserved. A crazed conservation that only promoted decay.

Standing in a clearing on the living-room floor, oppressed by the rubbish surrounding him, McCadden wondered, 'Has someone already talked to you about this problem?'

'I beg your pardon?'

'About the prowler.'

'Who would talk to me?'

'Some of the local guards?'

Newburn shook his head. 'No.'

'Right. Have you noticed anything unusual in the area the last few weeks?'

Newburn seemed to wait for clarification of the terms. He blinked a couple of times, but didn't answer.

'Any strangers around?' McCadden prompted.

Newburn got suddenly agitated, betraying an exposed nerve, a source of irritation. 'A lot of people drive down the track from the road,' he snapped. 'Particularly around this time of year, in summer. Day trippers. They shouldn't. As far as I'm aware, the track is not part of the public road system. It's private. They climb the fences to walk on the headland, trespassing on the farmer's land. They continue to do it. There's nothing to see. No beach. The headland is bleak and rocky.'

McCadden grimaced in sympathy, but explained, 'I was thinking more of the night.'

'Night?'

'Someone coming here when it's dark.'

Newburn stared at him, anxious now, and channelling his

uneasiness into his right hand, as it played with the wooden buttons on his brown cardigan. He said. 'You mean Mr Logan?'

'Who?'

'Arthur Logan. He's the only one I know who came down here after dark. But he's not a stranger.'

The name was familiar to McCadden. He'd asked Newburn to repeat it not because of his own ignorance, but because he was surprised.

Artie Logan, a middle-aged, Irish-American business executive from Boston, was the managing director of Lisenter (Ireland) Ltd, a subsidiary of the multinational pharmaceutical company whose successful Irish plant a couple of kilometres down the coast had brought prosperity to the area the last decade. Three weeks ago Logan had disappeared. It wasn't unexpected. The story was, he drank too much. The rumours about its cause ranged from embezzlement of company funds through gambling debts to feeding a cocaine habit. Something financial nudging him over the edge. No one had actually seen him take his sailing boat out from its berth in Dunmore East. But no one was surprised when his body became entangled in the nets of a local trawler and ended up with a pathologist in the local mortuary.

Accidental death? Suicide?

McCadden asked, 'When was the last time you saw Mr Logan down here?'

Newburn didn't understand. Or misheard the question. He said, 'He's dead now.'

'Yes, I know he's dead.'

'His funeral is tomorrow. He wanted to be buried here.'

'But when did you last *see* him?'

'A couple of nights before he disappeared.'

'Was he visiting you?'

'No. He was calling on Miss Shiels.'

'Right. Look, ah ... you don't strike me as the kind of man who pries into the affairs of others, Mr Newburn.'

'I don't.'

'You keep to yourself, follow your own interests. You have your curtains closed at night. Would that be fair?'

Newburn nodded, pleased by the portrait. 'Basically.'

'You won't mind me asking you. How do you know that Mr Logan was visiting Eleanor Shiels?'

Newburn smiled slightly. 'The first time he called on her, he knocked here by mistake. He didn't know which cottage she lived in.'

'When was that?'

'More than a year ago. Almost two.'

'Did you get to know him?'

'Well, we discovered things in common. Sometimes, if Miss Shiels wasn't at home, he waited for her here. We had tea, although he preferred coffee. He was American. And we talked.'

'About what?'

'We shared an interest in music.'

McCadden raised his eyebrows, mildly astonished. 'Rock?' he asked incredulously.

Newburn recoiled. 'No, no.'

'Well, I thought since Eleanor Shiels was once a rock star . . . '

'Baroque, Inspector. Bach, Scarlatti, Vivaldi . . . '

'Wasn't he into photography as well?'

'I have no interest in photography.'

'OK. But what about Mr Logan?'

'We never addressed the question.'

'Right. Has anyone questioned you officially since his body was found?'

'No.'

'They probably will. They'll probably ask you about his state of mind the last time you saw him. If he was depressed, suicidal.'

'He seemed quite normal.'

'How well do you know Eleanor Shiels, Mr Newburn?'

'Casually. As casual neighbours. We exchange pleasantries when we meet.'

'Has she ever mentioned a man named Tony Wallace? Or Rookie Wallace?'

'I don't think so, no.'

'Does the name mean anything to you?'

'Tony Wallace?'

'Or Rookie Wallace.'

'No.'

'Going back to our earlier topic ... You haven't noticed anyone around at night during the last week or so, have you?'

Newburn looked anxious again, worrying that wooden button on his cardigan once more. He said, 'If a car pulls up at night, of course its headlights are visible, even from behind the curtains.'

'Whose car? Mr Logan's?'

'No, no. The guard. I suppose he was here on business, really, responding to the reports of, ah ... well, as you said, a prowler ... '

'You're talking about Sergeant Mullaney, are you?'

'Is that his name?'

'So he says.'

'Well, yes, Sergeant Mullaney, then.'

'He hasn't introduced himself to you, has he?'

'No.'

'Right. There's another character I'm particularly interested in. He's a stranger here. A rough-looking guy, with a scar on his cheek. Have you come across him?'

'No.'

McCadden sighed his disappointment. 'OK,' he accepted. 'Well ... thanks for your time, anyway.'

'No problem,' Newburn assured him.

No problem, McCadden repeated irritably to himself. Eighteenth-century music, a tip head of memorabilia and contemporary cliché. *No problem?* Ten years ago, Newburn would've said, *you're welcome*, the native phrase indicating that knowledge was considered communal and sharing it was natural. Now co-operation seemed to be on the basis of personal convenience.

Disgruntled, McCadden left the cottage and hurried moodily towards his car, kicking a loose stone from under his feet along the way. The stone ricocheted off a pot-hole and jumped up to hit the Ford Mondeo, chipping a little metallic paint from the passenger door.

McCadden glanced at his watch as he sat in and started the engine. Already past eleven. The evening lost. The chance of a date passed up. And nothing to show for it.

Except questions.

four

The morning started damp again, a little cold, with a thick mist hanging over the coastline, threatening another gloomy day in what had been a disappointing August in the south-east.

Through the mist, they carried Artie Logan's coffin from the church in Dunmore East down the steps to the waiting hearse. The casket was draped with a stars and stripes. And a US Marine sergeant marched smartly behind it.

The mourners didn't linger on the steps outside the church. Shivering from the damp, they hurried to their cars, turned on their heaters and kept their engines running while waiting for the hearse to pull away.

From Dunmore, the cortège took a strange route to the nearby graveyard at Corbally church. Instead of following the signposts, it turned south, into even poorer visibility, and snaked along the narrow coastal road. Halfway there it took another detour, this time to visit a scattering of houses known as Portally village. And after that it stopped again beside a promontory fort at Swines Head and at a standing stone in Ballymacaw.

Sitting in the front passenger seat of an official car driven by a uniformed guard, McCadden wondered what the interruptions meant, what private associations were passing away with the dead man. He didn't ask. The driver was preoccupied with the road. And behind him Chief Superintendent Daniel Cody was sitting rigidly on the rear seat and staring sullenly out the side window.

Something troubling the Chief Superintendent this morning. Something fresh. And undigested.

The night before, when McCadden had contacted him with a request to attend the funeral, Cody had been touched by his own misreading of the suggestion. It was, he cheerfully admitted, the kind of public gesture he was addicted to, the kind of image he craved. The force as an integral element of a caring society, fighting the same struggles, suffering the same losses. Human. And vulnerable.

This morning, though, Cody was uncommunicative again. Almost resentful, in fact. Ignoring McCadden. And barking at the nervous young driver. 'Don't *attack* the bloody brake pedal, man!'

It was ten o'clock when they finally reached the graveyard at Corbally crossroads.

Brownstown Head was to the south on their left. Eleanor Shiels's cottage was less than four kilometres away. And the ubiquitous Sergeant Mullaney was already busy at the inter-section, furiously directing traffic on the tight roads and organizing parking around the junction. As the Chief Superin-tendent's car passed within centimetres of his toes, he comically attempted a parade-ground salute that his superior didn't even acknowledge.

McCadden sat on for a while once they'd parked, calculating a decent interval after the grumbling Cody had gone to jostle for his place in the pecking order of VIPs. By the time he finally left, the mist had lifted. The clouds were already breaking overhead and there was a promise of warmth in the air. But it was too late for most of the attendance. Unable to turn back, they were now stuck with their heavy greatcoats and their corporate umbrellas.

The church, huddled under the hills a short distance from the crossroads, wasn't open for the ceremony. Small and recently built, all dull plaster and plain glass, it seemed – from the outside at least – to have no architectural or historical interest. The graveyard behind it was older, its headstones an array of memorials to the Celts and Vikings, Normans and English, who'd once lived in or invaded or colonized this cramped corner of the country.

As always with country funerals, the mourners went at tangents for a while, visiting other graves and reminiscing about previous burials. Without attachments of his own, McCadden just drifted and watched, taking the central pathway through the cemetery and then slowly working his way back towards the road along a perimeter track to avoid getting caught in the crowds once the service started.

Artie Logan's plot was in the south-west corner of the grave-yard, under a low wall and next to the graves of three local fishermen lost on 4 February 1996, when the *Jenalisa* went down in a storm off Brownstown Head. The coffin, still draped in the American flag, lay on a trellis of boards, waiting to be lowered. Beside it, the US Marine still stood rigidly to attention.

The soldier was the most colourful of the impressive cast of mourners. Probably the most mysterious, too. But not the most surprising.

On the Marine's right there were three politicians, includ-ing Niall McAwley, the senior government minister who was McCadden's ultimate boss.

McAwley was a bantam man – five foot nothing and over-stocked with belligerence – who was much in the news at the time. His name kept cropping up at one or other of the judicial tribunals investigating corruption and graft and bribery and tax evasion among politicians. But the dirt wouldn't stick to him. The accusations never held. He seemed impenetrable. An old-fashioned hustler who'd slipped the net and adapted to change. A fibreglass dinosaur.

To the Marine's left, separated by a sleek, suntanned, athletic guy in his early sixties, there were a couple of film stars. One was Cathy Morrison, an Irish redhead who'd recently made it big enough in Hollywood to be recognized at home. The other was a clone, a plastic leading man who'd featured in a couple of recent blockbusters and whose agent, it was rumoured, was currently trying to coach him to deliver the line convincingly, *Are there parts that extend one any more?*

When the sun broke through – just as the priest opened the service by blessing the coffin – the clone was the only one to welcome its rays, turning his face slightly upwards to catch their warmth and adjusting his profile a notch to capture the most favourable light. *Those whom the cameras love, love themselves*, McCadden thought unkindly. Most of the others, still over-dressed and as badly shackled by convention as by buttons, just started to sweat. At first from the unexpected heat. And then from the embarrassment of appearing so gauche. Until they reminded McCadden of small children who hadn't made it to the toilet on time and who had to live as best they could with the mess.

He wondered if Artie Logan would've enjoyed the joke.

Looking at Eleanor Shiels, who was standing alone on the opposite side of the open grave, dressed in a lightweight black suit and wearing an expression of slight contempt on her face, he reckoned the man might have. If the pair had been as close as Sonny Newburn suggested. If they'd shared the same scepticism.

McCadden wasn't the only one closely studying Eleanor Shiels, though.

A couple of paces to her left, in the front row of the arc of mourners now pressed around the open grave, there was a small, bearded man, leaning against the low wall on the perimeter of the graveyard. Judging by the elevation of those around him, by the relative position of Niall McAwley, he seemed to be a little over five feet in height. But, unlike McAwley, he also had the stunted physique of a dwarf. A barrel chest. Rounded shoulders. Short arms and bowed legs.

He was staring intently at Eleanor Shiels. So intently that she sensed the attention and glanced up. He looked away in confusion, suddenly pushing himself from the wall and then self-consciously stooping a little to catch a whisper from the young brunette who was standing beside him. This second movement struck McCadden as comical. There was something in it, he thought, that betrayed the male's childish craving for superiority. Because the brunette was six or seven inches taller than the little man. And instead of bending, he'd have to stand on a low stool to comfortably reach her lips with his ear.

The expression on Eleanor Shiels's face didn't change. It was still ironical. Still mildly contemptuous. She kept looking at the bearded man for a while, until she was certain that she'd scared

22

him off, and then she went back to staring across the open grave at the glum politicians and the self-conscious film stars.

Oblivious to it all, the priest rambled on with the funeral service. His delivery without feeling. The formula without meaning. His words rising with the warm air and fading as they climbed, like bubbles idly blown by a child into the sky and then forgotten.

Easing out through the back of the dense crowd, McCadden found himself past the iron gates on the gravelled entrance to the graveyard again. From there he ran a last, leisurely check over the gathering. Sonny Newburn wasn't among the mourners, he confirmed. And neither was Rookie Wallace.

He turned away.

On the road behind him, Sergeant Mullaney was still in place. But the man was now so rigid that he seemed like a strange, neglected monument in the centre of a calmed traffic island. The daylight was kinder to his appearance, crueller on his personality. A physically imposing man, he came as close to being a giant as the bearded guy at the graveside was to a midget. But there was something unappealing about his rough, weathered face. It lacked complexity, McCadden decided. His eyes seemed capable only of the most simple emotions, passions that were basic enough to verge on the brutal. Lust and suspicion the previous night. Loyalty and servility now. His respect for authority was obviously deep. Unquestioned. And worrying.

'Would you like a cigarette, sir?' he asked as McCadden approached.

For a second, McCadden was completely thrown, wondering if the sergeant had reserves of irony that he hadn't even dreamed about. But the question wasn't a coded reference to the events of the previous night. Only an oily attempt at ingratiation.

McCadden shook his head. 'I'm giving them up.'

'Ah!'

'Since last night.'

'But would you mind if I, ah . . . ?'

'No.'

While the sergeant furtively lit up, McCadden gestured towards the funeral. 'How well did you know him?'

23

'Mr Logan, sir?' Mullaney hungrily sucked in smoke and then released it grudgingly while concealing the cigarette in his closed hand. 'He was well known around these parts.'

'Why the American flag?'

'He was in their army, I'm told.'

'Right.'

McCadden paused. Not to search for the next question. Just to vary the rhythm. To leave space for Mullaney's irritating efforts at smoking.

He asked then, 'Why wasn't the body brought back to the States?'

'He asked to be buried here. He bought that plot six or seven years ago now, a few years after he first came to work here. I don't think he had any family left in America. Brothers. Sisters. Anything like that. He was an only child, they say. The parents are dead a long time. And I don't think he ever married. No one came over from the States for the funeral. Except for Mr McMullan.'

'McMullan?'

The sergeant pointed with the butt of his cigarette before dropping the filter on the ground and crushing it under his enormous right boot. 'The white-haired man between the two actors, sir. He's the owner of Lisenter, where Mr Logan worked.'

'Who's the little guy with the beard?'

'That's Michael Constant. One of the locals. He owns the first bungalow on the headland, there.'

'And the girl standing beside him?'

'Ellen O'Doherty. Poor thing.'

'Are they together?'

'Oh, yes.'

'Do you know what their relationship is?'

The church bell tolled suddenly, its heavy clang reverberating across the quiet countryside, startling the mourners and disrupting the line of McCadden's interest.

A ripple of unease unsettled the crowd around the grave. Heads were raised, looking towards the belfry and towards the locked doors of the church. Hands were lifted to shield the eyes from the sun.

Thrown by the movement and the noise, the priest stuttered and coughed drily. He hurried through the few remaining prayers and then stepped back in confusion, tripping over someone's foot and staggering a few paces before being caught and rescued. He stood for a couple of seconds, struggling for composure, the eyes of his congregation on him again. Then he gestured impatiently at Bill McMullan.

McMullan hesitated. He glanced uncertainly between the cleric and the belfry. But the belfry was silent now. And the cleric importunate. So he stepped forward. He slipped a sheaf of notes halfway out of his overcoat pocket, but seemed to think better of adding to the awkward formality and decided to ad lib instead.

The casual style didn't sit too easily on him, though. Too many dollars had already been spent on his designer clothes. And too many more on his sculptured body. When he smiled, his teeth were just a shade too brilliant. And their excess drew attention to all his other artifices. You noticed, for instance, that his skin was too smooth. That his eyebrows were too neat. That his nose was probably a little too straight . . . All in all, he looked a little unreal. So unreal, in fact, that the plastic actor by his side might've been his natural son.

When he spoke, his voice was lively and upbeat, offering an almost provocative contrast to the dreary homily of the priest, but somewhat out of sync with the natural melancholy of the occasion.

Maybe he'd never really liked Artie Logan all that much, McCadden thought. Maybe he was determined to take death the American way. Open-faced and stoical, with his shoulders back. Or maybe he was just the archetype of the returning emigrant. *Exuding* success.

Whatever.

'Looking around at the crowds we got gathered here today,' he said, 'I guess Artie made himself just about as popular and as well respected here in Ireland as he had been back home. Myself, I've known this guy since we were kids in Boston. *Irish* kids, surrounded by Cavanaghs and Dohertys, Doyles and Driscolls . . . '

McMullan gradually warmed to his eulogy. But he also remained apprehensive.

Perhaps he was waiting for that bell to toll again, McCadden speculated. As if he suspected that the first chime hadn't been an accident.

The same edgy mood affected his audience as well. There was a sense of impatience about them. A distinct unease. An audible release of tension when McMullan wound up his shortened tribute and the priest stepped forward again with the final blessing.

Afterwards, the impassive Marine collected his country's flag. As he withdrew and offered a last salute, the undertaker's men lifted the casket and slipped away the boards that held it in place. Slowly they lowered the coffin into the grave, retrieved the ropes that were threaded through the handles, replaced the boards and rolled the prepared rectangle of green earth over the opening.

And nobody cried.

A child laughed briefly at the back of the crowd. And overhead, two seagulls started squabbling about a crust of bread.

And that was the only soundtrack Artie Logan was granted to ease him on his way.

Maybe tears would've unduly delayed the mourners, McCadden thought. And they *did* look anxious to get away. Most of them, anyway.

Eleanor Shiels stayed faithfully by the grave, her head bowed. For a few seconds, the little guy with the beard kept her distant company, staring across at her ... until the young brunette by his side suddenly slipped away from him and made a frantic dash towards the Hollywood stars.

She might've been a fan. She had that tortured expression on her pale face that marked off the true fan. Completely awestruck, but mixed with slight resentment, and tinged with the dread of rejection. Despite her credentials, she never quite made it, although Cathy Morrison saw her coming and clearly waited for her, indicating to the others that she'd follow them in a minute.

Michael Constant immediately felt the brunette's absence and surged after her, violently grabbing her arm and dragging her backwards. And for a few moments, beyond the bobbing heads and shoulders of the departing mourners, there seemed to be the promise of an awkward, unpleasant little scene.

Unfortunately, McCadden didn't catch the end of it. The distinctive sound of a pair of leather gloves being thwacked into the palm of an official hand sounded close to his right ear. And a second later the Chief Superintendent's formal voice made a proud announcement. 'I'll be travelling with the Minister, Inspector. Take the car back to the station when you're ready.'

Cody didn't wait for McCadden's congratulations. He couldn't afford to. Scurrying away in pursuit of the miniature politician, he made the back seat of the ministerial Mercedes just in time to be whisked away without breaking his legs.

McCadden turned to Sergeant Mullaney, intending to ask him what he'd meant by describing the brunette as a *poor thing* earlier. But Mullaney, too, was preoccupied by now. Back on point duty, he'd completely lost himself behind a flurry of arms and signals as he cleared the congested crossroads.

As McCadden watched, fascinated by the big man's exaggerated movements, the young brunette passed in front of him. Ellen O'Doherty was alone by then and obviously distressed, her right hand covering her mouth and nose, keeping the tears from flowing. Back in the graveyard, Michael Constant was sitting on the low perimeter wall, staring across at Eleanor Shiels, who hadn't moved from the buried coffin. They were the only two left by the grave.

'Sir?'

McCadden turned. The uniformed guard who'd been detailed as his driver for the day was shuffling about beside him, a look of bewildered distress on his young face. 'Yes?'

The driver swallowed hard and blurted out, 'I've lost the Chief Superintendent, sir.'

McCadden raised an eyebrow. 'It's not that difficult, surely? I've been doing it for years.'

'No, sir, I mean I can't find him and—'

'All right, all right. Don't worry about it. Did you find out where the wake is, by the way?'

'The local pub, sir, about a mile down the road. Is that where the Chief Superintendent is?'

'That's a good idea. Do you want to check it out? I'll meet you there. I've got to make a social call first.'

five

Michael Constant's bungalow, the first in the row of four on cramped plots at the entrance to the headland, was all plain grey concrete, dark grey slate and double-glazed PVC windows. Ugly to look at, even in brilliant sunshine. The kind of crude blot on a romantic landscape that provoked outraged criticism from environmentalists and dogged defence from people whose grandparents had died of hypothermia in more traditional cottages.

When McCadden reached it, after following Ellen O'Doherty on foot from the graveyard, the front door was still open. He knocked lightly and called in. 'Hello?'

The response from inside was instant. But the voice was strange. It sounded a little distorted. And the name it called wasn't fully articulated. 'Mi . . . ael?'

Before McCadden could answer, Ellen O'Doherty rushed to the door.

Up close, she looked older than she'd seemed at a distance. Late twenties, probably. She had a pleasant face, soft-featured, a little plump. But her eyes were disconcerting. Not only because they were reddened from crying, but because the expression died in them so quickly. At first bright and hopeful, they instantly became lifeless when they looked at McCadden. It wasn't a shift of mood. Wasn't disappointment. It was a blankness. An *emptiness*.

'Do I . . . know you?' she stammered.

And again, the delivery was defective. That same unnatural

break, this time in the flow of a short sentence, as if she could manage to talk only in very small units.

McCadden held his ID open in front of her, trying to gauge how much she understood. 'You probably don't know me,' he said. 'I'm a Garda inspector, from Waterford. My name's McCadden. Carl McCadden.'

'You want Mi . . . ael?'

'Well, no, not really.'

'Is he . . . in trouble?'

'No, it's nothing like that. I'm just making enquiries, that's all. Someone on the headland, you see, has complained of a prowler in the area.'

'Prow . . . er?'

'It may be nothing. But it may be a burglar, for instance, checking the dwellings. We don't know yet.'

She has no trouble absorbing information, he noticed. And very little *deciding* on a response. Her problem was communicating. 'Will you . . . come in?' she finally offered.

McCadden nodded and followed her when she turned. 'Thanks, yes.'

The interior of the bungalow was just as graceless as the outside. All dark colours and coarse fabrics. Past a small porch, there was a gloomy living room, bludgeoned by chunky oak furniture and killed off with brown upholstery and muddy paintwork. There were too many doors and they were too symmetrically arranged. It made the area feel like the lobby of a cheap hotel.

On McCadden's right, one of the doors was ajar. Through the gap he caught a glimpse of a small room and of a colourful display of photographs attached to the walls inside. He was drifting across, drawn by the sight of a familiar but unexpected image, when the brunette's voice, skirting that consonant in the middle of the name again, suddenly tugged him back. 'Mi . . . ael.'

McCadden turned sharply. 'Sorry?'

She tried to smile, but the words pursed her lips in the opposite direction. 'Be back . . . soon.'

'Oh, right.'

Ellen O'Doherty was extremely nervous. Not because she had a stranger in her house, McCadden thought. She needn't have invited him in. But because she was scared of assuming responsibility, of taking questions and supplying answers without Michael Constant's guidance.

Her inclination being to run and hide, she fell back on a stereotype, grasping at the traditional role of the rural Irish woman entertaining a visitor. 'I'll make . . . you tea.' Although in fairness, she also looked embarrassed as she offered, as if she was aware that her intelligence was superior to her nerves.

McCadden pretended not to notice her unease. 'That'd be nice,' he said. 'Thank you.'

When she drifted off, closing the kitchen door behind her, he hurried over to the room on his right and stood in the open doorway.

There was a light on inside.

And it was necessary, despite the midday sunshine. The heavy curtains on all the windows had been closed, giving the place a musty, secluded atmosphere.

The room had the basic furniture of a study. A desk. A cheap computer. A swivel chair. A couple of low bookshelves.

The photographs on the walls weren't all blown-up prints, as he'd first thought. Some were posters. A few were illustrations cut from magazines and newspapers. But otherwise his impression had been accurate. The entire wallspace facing the door, above the writing desk, was devoted exclusively to Eleanor Shiels.

This wasn't a secular shrine, though. It wasn't even a celebration of the singer's career. It was more a scrapbook of her weaknesses, her failures, her frequent lows.

The photographs, and the accompanying clippings, were all about thirty years old by then, from the heyday of her short career.

Most of them were cruel.

One particularly brutal image showed her drunk or drugged in London's Soho. It was from July 1974, when she was nineteen years old. In it, her long black hair was tangled and bedraggled. Her kid's face was drawn and pasty behind dark glasses. Her right foot was caught in a flapping plastic bag and slipping off the edge of the footpath. And her normally elegant body, about to fall on its face, was crumpled into an ugly, demeaning posture.

Under the headline CATCH A FALLING STAR, the report was prurient, gleeful. McCadden read it quickly, trying to remember what he'd been doing that distant summer's day, when he was fourteen years old.

> Outraged fans who bought the overpriced tickets and turned up at the National Stadium for the Edge Links concert, only to find the lead singer 'indisposed', were later disgusted to learn that Eleanor Shiels spent the evening mocking their stupidity in a London pub in the company of two notorious playboys. Fuelled with a lethal cocktail of drugs and booze, Shiels later collapsed on a Soho street. Not surprisingly, she was promptly abandoned by her beery knights. When she was later arrested and charged with being drunk and disorderly and in possession of illegal substances, she reportedly vomited all over the station desk . . .

There were other outraged reports. Other images of an entangled Eleanor Shiels. Other scathing headlines. But McCadden's attention was drawn away from them. The smaller wall surfaces to his right and left, he noticed now, also held crowded displays of photographs and press cuttings. Dedicated to different topics.

On his right the most prominent item was a black and white photograph of a dour old woman who was almost completely shrouded in a black shawl and posing reluctantly in front of the half-door of a thatched cottage. Above it there was the preposterous headline, THE MERRY WIDOW CONSTANT. There was no date. Judging by the clothes and the style of the cottage exterior, McCadden guessed that it must be about fifty years old, perhaps from the late forties or early fifties.

To his left there was a brief report on a proposed new pharmaceutical plant to be built in the area by the American corporation, Lisenter. It had been cut from a national newspaper about a decade earlier. Surrounding it were related items. An account of the factory's official opening. A critical article on the parent company from an American magazine. A pen portrait of its owner, Bill McMullan. An article from a medical journal raising fears about the side-effects of one of Lisenter's drugs.

McCadden glanced at both displays, but didn't get time to check the details of either. From behind, a deep, irritated voice violently accused him.

'Hey! You're trespassing, you!'

McCadden turned. Michael Constant was standing in the centre of the living room. His face was set with annoyance and all his visible muscles were tense and straining, as if he was about to launch an attack.

McCadden produced his ID again. And introduced himself again. But Constant wasn't impressed.

'Do you have a search warrant?' he demanded aggressively.

McCadden raised his eyebrows. 'Search warrant?'

'So you could legally come in here.'

'I think you might have the wrong idea, Mr Constant.'

'How would you know what idea I have?'

'It is Michael Constant, isn't it?'

'What do you want?'

'We're making enquiries. There have been reports of a prowler on the headland.'

'You don't fool me, you know.'

'I suppose I don't,' McCadden accepted. 'But have you seen any strangers about lately? Anyone acting suspiciously? I'm particularly interested—'

'Could you please get out of my house?' Constant interrupted. 'No one invited you in here.'

'Well, that's not true, actually.'

'No one who had the authority to invite you in.'

'Well, that's different.'

'I don't see anything different about it.'

'I thought Ms O'Doherty lived here, too. Does she?'

'That's not any of your concern.'

'Do you smoke, Mr Constant?'

'Why?'

'I've run out of cigarettes.'

'I don't smoke.'

'Not to worry. Would you apologize to Ms O'Doherty for me? Tell her I'll take that tea some other time.'

Constant didn't respond. He didn't waver in his pit-bull posture. He didn't even turn as McCadden wandered back towards the front door.

Maybe he'd carry the apologies to the nervous young brunette, McCadden thought. Maybe he wouldn't. Maybe she'd enjoy his style of relaying the message.

Or maybe not.

There seemed to be a coil of resentful aggression wound up inside the little man.

six

Someone was smoking dope at Artie Logan's wake.

As soon as he was inside the noisy pub, McCadden caught its distinctive, sweetish odour in the air, stronger than the usual smell of spilled beer and burning tobacco. He thought immediately of the butts in the soft earth outside Eleanor Shiels's cottage. And just as quickly he decided to let it drop. The pub was too crowded for a chase. The occasion all wrong. The chances of doing anything better than causing a row too remote.

Needing a drink, he pushed on through the packed mourners. But the bar was woefully staffed. Two flushed and sweating teenagers, both of them girls, were floundering under the sea of hands waving banknotes towards them and the babble of voices hurtling orders at them. Their incompetence was provoking arguments on the floor. A big, hard-boned farmer was squaring up to a plump little guy in a white cotton suit, accusing him of jumping the queue. And McCadden's uniformed driver was squeezed in between them, struggling to keep the peace.

McCadden used his ID to quickly reach the scene. But things had cooled again by the time he got there. The man in the white suit had disappeared. And the farmer was triumphantly clutching a pint of Guinness.

McCadden winked at the uniformed driver, leaned across the bar counter, tugged the sleeve of one of the passing teenagers and showed his badge. 'Double vodka and white lemonade,' he told her softly. 'When you're ready.'

His style drew down attention, of course. But most of it was fleeting. To the thirsty, the girls behind the bar were far more interesting than his sly manoeuvres. And McCadden was more envied than resented.

Only one of the customers retained an interest in him.

She was sitting on a high stool at the other end of the bar, surrounded by ancient admirers and slowly nodding her head at something a toothless old farmer was vigorously proposing, but her blue eyes were staring at McCadden.

He was flattered. His admirer was the red-headed actress, Cathy Morrison. And he was surprised to find her there. Her sidekick, the plastic he-man, had already split, adorning the more upmarket version of the wake at nearby Corballymore House, along with the Minister for Justice, the Chief Superintendent and Bill McMullan.

McCadden's enhanced self-esteem lasted about thirty seconds, until his drink was served. Turning to pay for the round, he caught a glimpse of Cathy Morrison instantly taking advantage of his distraction. As soon as his attention was diverted, she quickly dipped her head, furtively lifted a joint to her lips, and greedily sucked in smoke.

McCadden sighed. Realizing now that someone had warned her he was a cop and that while she was staring at him she'd been frozen by watchfulness, not fascination.

A little deflated, he abandoned his loose change on the counter. He mixed his drink, took a stiff shot from it, then turned and headed towards the end of the bar.

They saw him coming. Knew who he was. And fell silent.

He contemplated the strange group. This fabulous young woman, red hair cascading over naked shoulders, bare legs crossed under a blue leather mini, perched on a high stool and surrounded by grisly old countrymen in old-fashioned suits. A flash of erotic colour against an arc of grey.

She was the kind who attracted old men, he saw. The younger males kept a more careful distance, coveting from afar, scared of losing control and panting openly if they shuffled any closer.

When he reached the group, he offered his hand. 'Carl McCadden.'

She took it. Uncertainly. 'Cathy Morrison.'

He said, 'I always thought the standard cigarette was a better prop for an actress. Remember Lauren Bacall in *Key Largo*? Ingrid Bergman in *Casablanca*? The switch to the reefer in the sixties spoiled the effect. *Klute*, maybe? *Easy Rider*? Not the same . . . attraction.'

She crushed the joint she'd been smoking in an ashtray on the counter. Smiled uneasily. 'I'm not sure how I should take all that.'

'Why not?'

'Is it movie criticism? Morality? Image consultancy?'

McCadden shrugged. 'I don't suppose we're going to find a quiet corner to discuss it in here, do you?'

'Doubt it.'

'Would you like to go outside? There's no beer garden, as such, but there are some benches.'

'One of those offers you can't refuse,' she muttered.

She slipped from the bar stool, asked the old men to keep it free for her and promised to be back with them in a few minutes. McCadden stepped aside, allowed her to take the lead, knowing that the crowd would make her passage a lot more comfortable than his own. In fact, they parted in front of her like awestruck extras on the set of a biblical epic, registering her passing with orisons. 'There you are, Cathy!' 'Good girl, Cathy!'

The only delay came from McCadden's uniformed driver, who sidled up to him and whispered conspiratorially, 'Excuse me, sir, but if I'm not mistaken, someone on the premises is smoking can—'

'It's all right,' McCadden assured him. 'Have you found the Chief Superintendent yet?'

'No, sir.'

'Not to worry. Keep trying.'

A couple of kids, bored with burying the dead and now buzzing from too much caffeine in their cola, were running around wildly outside, chasing each other. McCadden dodged them and led the way to the rear of the pub.

Cathy Morrison placed her drink on a wooden table and sat on the bench attached to it, but facing McCadden, leaning back against the edge of the table. She crossed her legs. She took a packet of cigarettes and a silver lighter from her bag, flipped open the lid of the pack and offered its contents. 'Do you smoke?'

McCadden shook his head. 'No. Thanks.'

She slipped out a cigarette, rolled it gently between her fingers, moistened her lips before pressing them around the filter-tip. When she lit up, she deliberately evoked the style of the classic movies McCadden had mentioned. She didn't look at the flame being sucked on to the open tobacco. Her eyebrows raised, she stared at McCadden, watching his reaction.

Is that better? her performance seemed to ask.

But McCadden didn't respond and she quickly tired of the game. It was pointless without an audience. Halfway through, she finished with the cigarette, flicking it to the ground and crushing the stub under her heel. A little lost for a pose, she took a pair of Raybans from her bag and slipped them on against the sunlight, apologizing for concealing her eyes. 'Do you mind?'

Again, McCadden shook his head. 'No.'

She reached behind to take her glass from the table, but didn't drink from it. She pointed with it towards the slated roof of the pub. She said, 'That was thatched when I was a child. It looked magnificent. It's not the same now, is it?'

McCadden was surprised. 'Are you from this area?'

'I was born in Lismore. Do you know it?'

He nodded. 'Ecclesiastical town,' he recited. 'Famous for its monasteries and crosiers.'

'We always came to Tramore for our summer holidays when I was a kid. You can see the caravan park from here, just across the bay.'

'And you walked across the sand dunes when the tide was out, over to the headland here.'

'Sometimes.'

'Did you know Artie Logan?'

'He didn't live here then.'

'From your more recent visits.'

'Yes, I knew him. And you?'

'No, I never met him.'

'So what brings you to his funeral, then?'

'Oh, curiosity mostly.'

'About what?'

'The young woman who approached you at the graveside after the service,' McCadden said. 'Do you know her?'

Cathy Morrison looked at him sharply. Even from behind the Raybans, her anxiety was obvious. 'You're a policeman, aren't you?'

'Detective inspector.'

'Why do you ask? Is this some kind of official enquiry? Because we were told by the production company's head of security to direct everything through him.'

McCadden frowned. 'You've lost me,' he admitted. 'What production company are we talking about?'

'The film?'

'What film?'

More than anything else, his ignorance about her career seemed to annoy her. She snapped at him, 'Why the hell did you think we're all crowded into this little corner of the world? We're shooting a film here.'

'On the headland?'

'Yes, on the headland.'

'What's it called?'

'It's called *Sacrifice*.'

'What's it about?'

'I don't know.'

'You don't *know*?'

'I mean, I can't discuss it. I have to direct you to the publicity department.'

'Right. Fair enough.'

'We were told there might be some opposition to the location.'

'Is there?'

'I haven't noticed any so far. But it's why I wanted to know if your enquiry was official.'

McCadden sat down, on the same bench as Cathy Morrison, a little to her left. She swivelled slightly to keep facing him. He drank the last of his vodka, put the glass on the table.

'It's like this,' he explained. 'There's a possibility – and no more than a possibility – that there's a prowler in the area. Ellen O'Doherty would strike me as vulnerable. For that reason, I'd like to learn a little more about her.'

Cathy Morrison reached for another cigarette. But she smoked for herself this time, drawing in the nicotine for comfort. When she was calm again, she said, 'You're right. I know Ellen. I've known her for seven, eight years now.'

'From holidaying in the area?'

'No, we actually met at college in Dublin. We were both in the Drama Society.'

'She was an actress?'

'Pretty good, too.'

'The handicap is recent, then.'

'About eighteen months ago, I think. Less than two years, anyway.'

'What happened to her?'

'I'm not too sure. Not for certain. Apparently she was on some adventure expedition with a works group.'

'From the theatre?'

'No. I think she was trying to supplement her acting. Summer work. Anyway, she fell from a cliff. It was in the papers at the time.'

'Were you close to each other?'

'Not really, no. Coming from the same country area and meeting by accident in Dublin, there's a connection, obviously ... But I went to the States after college and she stayed here. I was kind of lucky, I suppose. I got the breaks. We wrote back and forth a couple of times, but nothing more than that. And it dried up pretty quickly.'

'Why was she so anxious to talk to you today?'

'Yeah, well ...'

'It seemed to me more than just a desire to renew an old acquaintance.'

'I don't think she has any memory of the accident and I don't think she understands the extent of her injuries. She remembers her acting career, though, and she still hopes to renew it. I'm a way back, I suppose.'

'But that's impossible, surely?'

'Obviously.'

'Do you know the man she was with today? Michael Constant?'

'I met him once before. I don't like him.'

'Why not?'

'I think their relationship is unhealthy.'

'Why?'

She shrugged. 'Personal opinion? On the basis of a single meeting? He's a control freak. She's desperate. It's a bad combination. I should know.'

McCadden fell silent, considered the personal invitation in that last statement.

Some of the others from the wake had spilled out of the pub by then, but they were still around the front of the building. Their laughter was distant.

He said, 'I've probably ruined your drink.'

She shook her head. 'No, not my drink.'

'Your appreciation of sixties movies, then.'

'It's as good a euphemism as any, I suppose.'

'What *are* you drinking?'

'Whiskey. On the rocks. Red lemonade.'

'Can I get you another? I'll let you enjoy it this time.'

'Not by myself, I hope?'

He grimaced at her. 'I think the prospects of you being left by yourself around here are slim, don't you?'

seven

Seven o'clock the next morning, an hour before the alarm was due, McCadden woke – *half*-woke – with the smell of dope in his nostrils. Confused, and still groggy, he drifted for a while between dreams and nightmare. He drowsily imagined the strands of Cathy Morrison's dark red hair spread out on the pillow beside him while she languidly smoked a joint. But when he reached out to touch her he scattered the image with his hand, revealing behind it a huge and menacing figure who was coldly observing him from a dark and bloodied background, and also drawing on a joint.

He woke fully then, jerking upright in the bed, where he sat rigidly. At first panting uncontrollably, he struggled afterwards to hold his breath and to listen for the sounds of the intruder he sensed.

Wood creaked as it expanded from heat somewhere in the house. Swallows dipped into the eaves outside his bedroom window.

But nothing else.

Sweating heavily, he pulled back the single sheet he'd been sleeping under and swung out of bed. He padded carefully down the steep wooden stairs from the loft to the flat's living room, still carrying the apprehension with him, even though he was assured now that the scares, and the smell of dope, were all inside his head.

He showered, dressed, laid out a breakfast of fresh coffee, toast, cereal; but touched only the coffee. And all with a muzzy, dislocated sensation, as if he was dulled by a hangover.

His head never cleared all morning. He just wasn't with it. He drove clumsily to work. He sat stupidly behind his desk and stared at the one brief report without ever grasping its contents. He heard things through a fog. And only sometimes answered. He took a return call from a second-hand record dealer named Mak McLeod offering the background on Eleanor Shiels he'd asked for, but was too slow to absorb the information and suggested visiting the shop instead. And about noon, when the big, lumbering detective sergeant, Frank Ryan, waddled across and tossed an open newspaper on the desk, with the inevitable grease stain from one of Ryan's doughnuts working its way inwards from a corner, the smell of dope came back to trouble him.

'Frank?' he asked.

'Uh-huh?'

'Do you get a distinct smell . . . ?'

'Smell? Of what?'

'No, never mind.'

'Doughnuts?'

'Don't worry about it, Frank.'

'I've just been eating doughnuts.'

'That's probably it, then.'

'We're heading out for something to eat. You want to join us?'

'No, no . . . '

'I'll catch you later, then. OK? We all want to know what the story is.'

'Story?'

McCadden had a forgettable lunch, alone. Drove to the court-house to give evidence in a burglary case. Drove back when he was belatedly informed that the trial was deferred because the book of evidence wasn't complete. Sometimes troubled by the smell of hash. Sometimes not. And wondering if he was taking the strain these days with the same margin of comfort he used to.

By the time Ryan got back to him, a little after two, he'd completely forgotten about their earlier exchange. The sergeant's monosyllabic reminder meant nothing to him.

'Well?'

'Well what?'

'Is it true?'

'Is what true? What are you talking about, Frank?'

'Did you read the report?'

'No. What report?'

Ryan searched. Across the surface of the desk. On the surrounding floor. He found the newspaper inside a brown folder. It was still opened on the page he'd selected earlier. He folded it twice to isolate an item and handed it to McCadden.

McCadden read. Slowly.

Under the headline, MURDER SQUAD BACK, there was a brief report.

The Minister for Justice, Mr Niall McAwley, is expected to announce the re-establishment of the Murder Squad within the Garda Síochána over the next few weeks. The famous squad, controversially disbanded in the eighties, will resume its role as an elite unit with exclusive responsibility for investigating homicides throughout the state. It will be staffed by officers who already have wide experience of murder investigations and will be located at Garda Headquarters in the Phoenix Park, Dublin. According to insiders, the early front runners for the prestigious job of heading the new unit are Superintendent Joe Havelin, of the National Bureau of Criminal Investigation, Inspector Tom Reynolds, Special Branch, and Inspector Carl McCadden, Head of Detectives, Waterford District . . .

Pressure to re-form the squad has grown in recent years due to the high level of unsolved murders, particularly of young women. The tide has swung again in favour of those who argue that separate investigations in different districts, often commanded and pursued by officers with little or no homicide experience and hampered by internal rivalries, are not only a wasteful duplication of resources, but also diminish the chances of establishing links between the deaths. The possibility that a serial killer is active in Ireland, preying on vulnerable young women in a variety of locations, has haunted senior figures in the Garda and the Department of Justice, and terrorized the public . . .

McCadden read it again, frowned, looked up at the expectant Ryan. He shook his head. 'I haven't heard anything.'

'Yeah, well, I know there's no *official* word yet,' Ryan accepted.

'No. On the level, Frank. I really haven't heard. Official. Unofficial. Shortlists. Rejections. I haven't heard.'

'But you did apply for it?'

'Yeah, I put in an application.'

'And would you take it?'

'Take it?'

'The job. If it was offered. Head of the Murder Squad.'

'Of course I'd take it, Frank. I wouldn't have applied otherwise.'

'Then you'd better polish up your acceptance speech. The superintendent's looking for you upstairs. And he's just after taking phone calls from the Minister and the commissioner.'

Cody was standing at the window in his office, his back to the door, looking out on the car park. His hands were stuffed inside his trouser pockets, lifting the rear flaps of his uniform's jacket. An unlit pipe was clenched between his teeth.

He didn't answer when McCadden knocked. And he didn't turn as the door was opened. Watching his visitor's reflection in the window pane, he said sharply, 'Sit down, Inspector.'

McCadden sat, gauging the colour of Cody's humour from the level of formality in the address. The man was irritated, tense, a little sullen. But it was nothing new, nothing you could read your future in. He'd been off form since the funeral the previous day.

Cody said nothing more for a long time. Even when he turned and joined McCadden at the desk, he only fidgeted with the pipe he took from his mouth, cleaning the bowl and pressing fresh tobacco into it. But eventually he coughed and muttered, 'I understand you know Cathy Morrison, Inspector?'

McCadden frowned. Knocked off balance, he was caught between surprise and wariness. 'Cathy Morrison?

'She's an actress. She was at the funeral yesterday. For some reason she didn't attend the function in Corballymore House afterwards, but you might have noticed her.'

McCadden nodded cautiously. 'Yes, I saw her there.'

'You might also have heard that they're shooting a film in Brownstown.'

'I think it's called *Sacrifice*, is it?'

'*Sacrifice*,' Cody confirmed. He sighed heavily, looked into the bowl of tobacco cupped by his hand and then opened a drawer and put the pipe away. 'The project has run into trouble locally. A few of the residents are opposed to it. Not many. A tiny minority, in fact. But the issue has now attracted outsiders, who've also taken it upon themselves to intervene. The pity of it is ... they've been there for three weeks and are leaving this Friday. The situation had been calm, with any objections verbally expressed. But that's now changed.'

'In what way?'

'Last night Miss Morrison was assaulted.'

McCadden pulled himself upright in the chair, an uneasy feeling in his stomach. 'How badly?' he asked.

'The local sergeant,' Cody went on. He stopped, flicked through papers he dragged towards him with his left hand. 'Mullaney,' he read. 'He was called to the scene after a passer-by found Miss Morrison unconscious. She'd recovered by the time he arrived. The film company are not too anxious to publicize the assault, but it's a Garda matter now and not for them to decide how it should be treated.'

'The actress,' McCadden asked again. 'Was she badly injured?'

'She was detained overnight in hospital for observation. She was released this morning. Could you manage to get out there before five this afternoon?'

'I reckon so, yes.'

'She *asked* for you, apparently.'

'Asked for *me*?'

'By name.'

'Right. Well, I actually met her after the funeral yesterday, although—'

'Her request went all the way up to the top, Inspector, and all the way back down again. I had a phone call about it from the commissioner's office this lunchtime. Just as I was leaving to meet my wife. The commissioner had taken a call from the

Minister's office. I suppose you saw the Minister for Justice at the funeral as well.'

'I noticed him, yes.'

Cody joined his hands in a bridge, leaned on the desk and released all his exasperation into the cold look he gave McCadden. 'He's a friend of the film's producer, Bill McMullan. Apparently, his party's ambition is to return a second candidate from this constituency at the next election. The film, along with McMullan's pharmaceutical plant, employs a lot of people in the area.'

McCadden raised an eyebrow. 'Right . . . '

'That'll be all, Inspector,' Cody told him. The tone was icy now, dismissive. 'Make sure you get to Brownstown by five, will you? Something to do with their shooting schedule, apparently.'

'Right . . . '

eight

Mak McLeod, in his mid-fifties, was a throwback to a looser age. A tall matchstick of a man in baggy blue jeans and purple grandad shirt, with a flowing grey beard and bobbing ponytail, he had so much facial hair that his bright blue eyes looked like a predator's watching from a bush.

His small shop, surrounded on the High Street by fast food joints, computer stores and boutiques, also seemed like a throwback. He had a photograph on the wall inside, showing the street as it had looked more than thirty years earlier. His was the only unchanged exterior, apart from the hand-painted sign showing the name and the trade. Back then, it had been a family bakery.

The story was that some developer was trying to move him on. Part of a crusade to give a pleasing consistency to the plastic façades along the row. But his lease was secure and he was dogged, uninterested in money and unmoved by corporate pressure.

Inside the shop, the fittings were basic. McLeod sat behind a high counter at the back, elevated above the commerce. At least, that must've been the original intention. But he wasn't the distant type, despite his eyes. He was too passionate about his subject. Most of his time was put in on the floor of the shop, occupying the same level as his customers and rooting with them through the mix of wooden and cardboard trays that held the huge collection of vinyl LPs, EPs, old 45s and tapes, covering every genre of twentieth-century music, every style, every period.

Business was always done on a leisurely basis. No one ever

came in, asked for an album and got only what they wanted. McLeod didn't recognize the unconnected event. Every song had a context, he insisted. And every context was worthy of discussion.

When McCadden got there that afternoon, it was a little after three and he was already watching the clock. McLeod was occupied. An intensely serious old man, holding his dog's leash in one hand and leaning on a walking stick with the other, was searching out an early recording of Fats Domino.

McCadden decided to give it five minutes, started browsing to kill the time, came across Ewan MacColl's *The Manchester Angel*, picked up a 1967 Danish recording of Sandy Denny and the Strawbs, reckoned he should buy them both and lost track of the time.

Eventually, he was startled by McLeod's interjection.

'A couple of other early MacColl albums from Topic I can get for you, if you like.'

'What?'

'If you're collecting him. Ewan MacColl?'

'Right . . . '

'They brought out a compilation of Sandy Denny on compact disc a couple of months ago, by the way. But you don't want that. I don't sell them. CDs lost the argument in this shop a long time ago. Sterile. No surface noise. No background noise. Sterile environment. Typical of our society. Terrified of AIDS. Obsessed with germs. Unhealthy. Drifting towards the barren. I haven't seen you here before. You new in town?'

Although badly tempted by the scattering of bait, McCadden managed to keep it simple. 'I'm Carl McCadden. I was talking to you on the phone this morning.'

McLeod's eyes lit up. 'Right! The Eleanor Shiels man. Funny thing. You hear nothing about an artist for years, and suddenly they're coming at you from all angles. What is it with you guys? You starting a fan club or something?'

McCadden was so surprised that he made a mistake. Instead of threading the query through the conversation, he blurted it out. 'Guys?'

McLeod was sharp. Immediately wary, he sensed an agenda

here other than the music. He said cautiously, 'Yeah. You're the second query I've had about Eleanor Shiels the last month.'

'Who was the first?'

McLeod smiled. 'Hey, ah . . . I think I better take a rain check on that one.'

'Come on,' McCadden argued. 'It's music we're talking about, not a confidential credit rating.'

'Still, you're a cop, aren't you?'

'Yeah, I'm a cop.'

'And I've got a reputation to keep. In here, the gossip sticks to the music.'

McCadden nodded. 'OK. That's fair enough, I suppose. What've you got for me, anyway?'

'You wanted some history on Eleanor Shiels?'

'As a short cut. Instead of trawling through old newspapers. Nothing that's not in the public domain.'

McLeod laughed and turned. He lifted the counter flap, reached behind into a pigeon-hole and came back with an LP and a cassette. The album was Eleanor Shiels's 1972 debut, *Dead Certain*. Its sleeve had a black and white photograph of the singer in that famous pose, that sideways glance across the naked shoulder.

'I got this for you,' McLeod explained. 'They never made a cassette of it. I put it on a tape so you can play it in the car. I can get the rest. The other solo album. The two she cut with Edge Links. There's a couple of contacts tracking them down for me. Two weeks. Maybe a month at the outside. You said you wanted some background on her. How much do you know?'

'The memories are blurred. I was fifteen when she packed it all in in 1975.'

'Fifteen? A year younger than Eleanor Shiels herself when she left for London in early seventy-one, carrying an old Gibson guitar and not much else. She did the folk clubs over there. Made a name for herself. Cut a couple of solo albums. Got a lot of air time on Radio One. Early seventy-three, she met Dave Pennick. Pennick played fiddle, viola, guitar, mandolin . . . anything else he could get a tune out of. He had a drummer, a bass guitarist, a lead guitar as well. More important, he had real talent as an arranger and producer. And that's where the band, Edge Links, started, when Eleanor Shiels's career took off. Their style married rock and Irish folk and traditional. All the buzz back then. The numbers she did got harder, more political, more radical, more personal at the same time. Mostly, they were cover versions. Some traditional, like "Barbara Allen". Some contemporary, like Richard Thompson's "No Man's Land". But the lyrics she did herself were better. I mean, better for her. No one remembers them now. If she's remembered at all, she's a singer, not a songwriter. You know "My Old Man Shot Me With A Camera"?'

McCadden shook his head. 'No.'

'One of hers. Quirky, but black, like all the rest of them. A teenage girl is photographed by her old man in an uncharacteristic pose. Except it's a conventional image the old man finds appealing. And the image is made permanent when the negative is developed. The snap isn't real. One moment out of a life. But it hangs around the kid's neck until she can't take it any more and she sticks a pistol between her lips and pulls the trigger. But of course, it was the camera shot her.'

'Restriction seems to be a concern of Eleanor Shiels.'

'It was a theme, sure. Right through her writing. Not the usual teenager's idea of a cage. You know. Poppa in the woodshed, Momma in the kitchen, preacher in the pulpit and the copper on your doorstep. More subtle. The stuff that fucks with your mind. Photos. Poses. Images. Album sleeves. Her recordings, stage numbers, they got more radical, more political, but her personal life went in the opposite direction. There was always that division. The cracks started to show even before the series of big concerts, even before she became big news. They intensified after, obviously. How do you solve it? She started not to show for concerts. One absence in seventy-five turned permanent. She just disappeared. Didn't surface again for years, when things had moved on without her, the punters had forgotten her. It's still a mystery. To me, anyway. No one I've ever met knows where she went.'

A couple of customers had come into the shop, drifted up and down a few times and were now impatient for attention.

McCadden's wristwatch bleeped, warning him it was four o'clock and he had less than an hour to make it to the film set in Brownstown. And he was still reluctant to drag himself out of Eleanor Shiels's fascinating history.

Until McLeod clicked back into selling mode.

'You want to take the *Dead Certain* album? I've thrown in the tape just for your personal use.'

'Yeah, thanks . . . '

'And the Ewan MacColl and Sandy Denny?'

'Yeah, I'll take those, too.'

'You want me to buy in the other Eleanor Shiels albums?'

McCadden had parked on Merchant's Quay, a short walk from McLeod's shop. When he got back to the Mondeo, he sat in, turned the key in the ignition, slipped the cassette into the tape deck and listened to the opening track while the engine was idling. 'The First Time Ever I Saw Your Face'. It was a pretty conventional treatment of the love song. And the guitar was no more than adequate. But the voice was great. Clean and clear. And strong enough to move the listener without straining.

He pulled out into the early rush-hour traffic, swinging right into Barronstrand Street, listening as he went. 'Running From Home' was up second. Followed by 'She Moves Through The Fair'. And there was the same feel to each of the numbers. The same sense of a major talent not really finding an individual style yet.

A local traffic jam, caused by a minor accident on Broad Street, took McCadden's mind off the music. He'd wormed free of the tailback, using a uniformed guard who'd come on the scene, and was pushing on down Michael Street, intent on making the green light at the junction ahead, when he was distracted again. He thought at first it was just another of those fuzzy dislocations he'd been suffering from all day. Only the trigger wasn't dope this time.

Overtaking a wobbling cyclist, he glanced in his left wing mirror to check that he was clear, and saw for an instant, before he had to switch his attention to the front again, a rough, familiar figure standing at the entrance to a fast food joint and looking furtively around. A big man. Big build. Dark hair. And a raw-looking scar on his left cheek.

Rookie Wallace?

McCadden braked hard. Unfortunately, a showy young learner was in his slipstream. And the learner was too close. He reacted late, swerving first, before panicking and slamming on the brake pedal. He was immediately into a skid, had his front passenger door sliding towards a collision with the Mondeo's tail lights, until McCadden accelerated away from contact and pulled into the footpath out of range.

The car behind was twelve years old, McCadden calculated. The worst combination on earth, he thought. A young male learner in a beat-up banger. So much to prove to the world and so unfairly handicapped, even with testosterone in the tank.

The kid got righteously out of his super-mini after dragging it to a halt in the centre of the road without touching anything. 'What the fuck—'

McCadden flashed his ID at him on the way past. 'Shut up,' he advised. 'And move on.'

Wallace, as far as he could gather – if it *had* been Wallace – was wearing a dark green shirt and black jeans. Not inconspicuous. But not exactly unique, either.

He wasn't standing in front of the restaurant any more. And, paradoxically, it was his *absence* that really convinced McCadden that he'd been there.

Wallace had heard the squeal of rubber, McCadden guessed. Looked up. Reckoned there was hassle coming his way. And split. Unlike everyone else in the area, including the old American couple standing beside him, who'd all been drawn towards the incident, all sucked in by the melodrama. Because none of *them* had anything to run away from.

McCadden pushed through the circling crowd, his hopes fading. He had a one in four chance of picking the right route at the junction itself. And the odds got worse with every little side street Wallace might've taken after that. Until the probability of even *seeing* a dark green shirt was dipping towards zero.

Frustrated, McCadden wandered back to the parked Mondeo. The kid in the ailing super-mini had wised up and left. Most of the crowd had dispersed. A small knot of dogged adventurers, intent on sustaining the drama, were busy contradicting each other's accounts on the footpath.

McCadden sat in the car. The engine wasn't running any more, but the ignition was still on. The Eleanor Shiels tape had reached the end of the album's first side and was spitting out static. McCadden ejected it, turned it over and rewound. He checked his watch and saw that he had only thirty minutes now to be punctual on set, as the Minister for Justice would've desired, and consequently the commissioner, and his own Chief Superintendent.

As he started the car, the cassette finished rewinding and clicked into play mode.

The first track on the flip side was 'The Night Before Larry Was Stretched'.

nine

For their three-week shoot in the area, the production company filming *Sacrifice* had rented the use of the public car park at the entrance to Brownstown Head from the local authority.

McCadden got there with five minutes to spare on his deadline.

The car park itself, crammed with trucks and tents and caravans, was the scene of some hectic, but fairly organized activity. The beach and sand dunes beyond it were both deserted for the moment. But the entrance to it – from a narrow, sloping lane leading in off the main road – was just chaotic.

A file of young picketers, all of them dressed in combat fatigues, military boots and balaclavas, was marching aggressively up and down, chanting violently. To McCadden, they looked like movie extras at first. Looked unreal enough and overstated enough to be part of a film. But their costumes were all wrong. The actors were *inside* the car park and wearing gear from the fifties. Or, at least, what Hollywood imagined the Irish to have worn in the fifties. Worsted woollen trousers, woollen waistcoats, peaked caps and the occasional polka-dot handkerchief tied jauntily around the muscular neck of some young buck.

Besides, the placards that the protesters were wielding were all scathing about the medium of film. THE CAMERA ROBS OUR SOULS, claimed one, echoing both a primitive belief and the subject of the Eleanor Shiels song McCadden had just heard described. Others were more direct. PILLAGERS OUT. NO EXPLOITATION. SANCTUARY, NOT IMAGES.

If that had been all, McCadden might've negotiated the obstacle, finished his business and checked on the cause of the protest on his way out. But there were other elements present and the mix was getting volatile. The film company's security staff seemed intent on provoking confrontation, edging forward to squeeze the protesters into a dangerously shrinking space. And there was a counter-picket of locals, more interested in abusing the protesters than in making a point of their own, raucously encouraging the security staff to claim more ground and goading them whenever they eased up a little.

The only barrier between the factions was the omnipresent Sergeant Mullaney and a nervous young guard beside him.

McCadden summoned the sergeant, indicated the protesters and raised a questioning eyebrow.

'They're from Dublin, sir,' Mullaney offered, as if that got to the bottom of their delinquency.

'Right. But who *are* they?'

'They're the ones who call themselves eco warriors. Some of them came from the motorway protest in the Glen o' the Downs. They came down last night and set up here.'

'Why?'

'The dunes there, sir, the Tramore Burrow, it's a bird sanctuary. Its protection is all being taken care of in the agreement with the film people, but the protesters don't accept that. They say the sanctuary is being destroyed. Nobody else agrees with them. And as you can see, sir, the locals don't want them.'

Well, they wouldn't, McCadden thought. The protesters were probably students, probably penniless, and certainly not carrying any corporate dollars to make their idealism more appealing.

He didn't share his scepticism. He said, 'I want a representative of the protesters over here, along with a representative from the local community. Only one of each. And the film company's head of security.'

The protesters' representative, when she pulled off her balaclava, turned out to be a beautiful young blonde whose smile would always win a lot more arguments than her rhetoric. She was the least likely looking warrior McCadden had ever seen in his life, although he didn't articulate such a grossly incorrect sentiment. And just for balance, the community's rep was a dry old gentleman who kept threatening the modern world with his walking stick.

The film company's head of security took longer to attract to the negotiations. But when he did appear, escorted by one of his staff from a caravan in the car park and past the outer barrier, McCadden's optimism sank a little.

It was another familiar face. Another troublesome history.

The man's name was Paul Hyland, a former detective sergeant. A guy who'd rescued and abandoned McCadden in about equal measures over the years. Charming. Irresistible. And totally undependable. Festooned with gambling debts, sexual affairs and dubious associates, he'd left the force about six months earlier, probably just ahead of a damning internal enquiry, and had obviously landed on his feet again.

Luckily, he didn't play for any advantage from knowing McCadden. He kept his mouth shut, nodding agreement.

'Whatever your boundary agreements are with the local authority,' McCadden told him, 'you place the barrier there and keep your staff behind it. As for the rest of you ... don't encroach. You're all entitled to peacefully make your case ...'

The point of the lecture wasn't to guarantee order. Words alone would never manage that. It was demarcation, a clarification of what was acceptable and what was potentially unlawful. Something for everyone to think about for a while. Something to weaken the ugly mood.

Walking with Hyland afterwards towards Cathy Morrison's caravan, McCadden glanced back and counted the number of eco warriors. 'Nine immediate suspects for the assault,' he suggested.

Hyland shook his head. 'No.'

'You don't think they're capable of it? Fervour finds some rough outlets at times.'

'I think someone else did it.'

'Oh? Who?'

Hyland didn't answer. He tugged McCadden's sleeve and said quietly, 'I'll talk to you later. On your left. Smile when you notice him.'

McCadden looked and saw the burnished American Bill McMullan, dressed in green check slacks, green shirt and white jacket, standing under the awning of a small tent and waving across at them.

McMullan bellowed. 'Mr McCadden!'

Like a model on remote control, Hyland veered immediately, tugging McCadden with him. McMullan strode to meet them, still calling. A loud man. Brash. Conscious of his own power. And pumping McCadden's hand with the same excessive vigour that he spilled compliments from his mouth.

'Good to meet you, Mr McCadden. Been hearing your name since I got here. Your Minister's hot on you just now, tells me you're in line for promotion. I guess you know that Niall's an old sparring partner of mine . . . '

Like most cops, McCadden disliked people who insisted on making the running in conversation. And effusive praise always made him jumpy.

He didn't much take to Bill McMullan. As the three of them turned again and headed back towards Cathy Morrison's private caravan, he decided that there was something phoney about the man. Something more than the surface vanity, deeper than the cosmetic surgery.

The actress was with a couple of make-up artists, a wardrobe assistant, a junior PA and the film's fretting director.

The production was already slightly behind schedule because of the death of Artie Logan. The assault on Cathy Morrison had knocked it even further back. So with a couple of hours' sunlight left in the day, they were still desperately trying to mask the damage to her face.

There was extensive bruising and swelling on her left cheekbone. The skin was puffed and broken in places, forcing the eye halfclosed. Ice packs and time would bring it down, McCadden thought, but right then there wasn't really much hope of using her in front of a camera.

The film's director, Bob Bettesworth, a slight, agitated Englishman, kept nattering constantly as the others worked, assuring her that they could easily rejig the schedule, shoot the scenes she wasn't featured in, use a stand-in . . . More desperate to convince himself than her.

Cathy Morrison looked up as McCadden came in with the others. She greeted him with an embarrassed smile. Apologizing for being a victim. 'Hi.'

Maybe it was McMullan's presence unsettling her, the sense he gave out that his dollars were burning with her idleness. He liked to make it known that he was bankrolling this effort. Even his quick departure now, hustling everyone else out before him, stressing the confidentiality of the interview between victim and policeman, made it obvious that he was in charge. His absence was a favour granted.

When they were alone, McCadden cupped her chin in his hand, gently turned her face to look at the wound and grimaced.

'Ugly,' she said.

'Anything broken?' he wondered.

'No. But ugly.'

He nodded sympathetically.

The light was dull in the caravan. She had the curtains closed. So it took him another minute or two to fully adjust after coming in from the glare of the sun and being granted relief from the more dazzling glitter of Bill McMullan. Then he pulled a chair out from the table and sat.

'What did the hospital say?' he asked.

She shrugged. 'When the X-rays showed up clear, they worried about concussion. I knew I hadn't been concussed. I was more concerned . . . I needed them . . . What frightened me was the possibility of a sexual assault.'

'What prompted you to worry about that?'

She looked quickly away from him. 'It's the sort of thing that occurs to you', she snapped, 'when you regain consciousness with your clothes in disarray.'

'It's just that nobody said anything about it before. *Was* there any evidence of sexual assault?'

Again, her answer was short and irritated. 'No.'

He said quietly, 'Would you prefer to talk to a woman detective?'

She shook her head. 'No.' She paused, clenching her fist a couple of times while regaining control. Dressed in costume – a light summer dress with a floral pattern in the style of the fifties – she looked more vulnerable than she would've usually. She said, 'When the guy grabbed me, the attack seemed like it was sexual at first. He approached from behind. I didn't hear him. He put his left hand over my mouth, his right hand all over the front of my body. I could feel his breath and I could hear him laughing in my left ear.'

'Did he have a beard?'

'What?'

'You probably felt his face touching against yours. Did you notice if he was bearded? Clean-shaven?'

She thought about it. 'I don't think he was bearded.'

'Smooth?'

'I'm not sure. But not bearded. There was something cold when he laughed in my ear.'

'Cold? His voice?'

'No, no . . .'

'His breath?'

'Something *solid*. A piece of jewellery. Or maybe just his lips or his teeth. I don't know.'

'Any other impressions? Tall or short? Reaching up or down to hold you? Strong or weak grip? Young or old voice?'

'I don't know. He seemed tall. He seemed strong. But most men would, wouldn't they, in a situation like that. He didn't talk. How do you judge the age of a laugh?'

'Do you remember being hurt?'

'No.'

'I don't think it's from a blow, is it? The position is all wrong. Someone would have to strike you while facing you. Did you fall?'

'I fainted.'

'When?'

'Pretty much as soon as he grabbed me, I think.'

'So he was still holding you?'

'Yes.'

'Where did it happen?'

'In the graveyard. Where the funeral was yesterday.'

'What time?'

'About midnight, I reckon.'

'Do you mind me asking you? What—'

'I was a little drunk by then.'

'Right.'

'Friends of mine, from when I was a kid coming here on holidays, they're buried there. I was maudlin, I guess.'

'Right. Were you alone?'

She nodded. 'I was stupid, wasn't I?'

'No . . .'

'But you mentioned yesterday that there was a prowler in the area.'

'Tell me what you did after I left you in the pub.'

'That was what? About noon? I had lunch in the pub. We were back on set about two, working all afternoon, into the evening. Most of the cast and crew went straight to Corbally-more House. It's where we're staying. I went back to the pub. You know, people there I hadn't seen for years. I suppose I drank too much. Eleven-thirty or so, I left, by myself. I walked back along the road towards Corballymore House. And I went into the graveyard as I was passing it.'

'Did you get a sense of anyone watching you at any time?'

'Watching?' she repeated. Her voice was incredulous. It wasn't vanity, just a pained reminder that she made a living from being watched.

'I know it sounds obvious,' McCadden accepted. 'But I don't mean admiration, curiosity, interest. I mean, the kind of watching that makes you uneasy. Any sense of someone *following* you?'

'I didn't notice anything.'

'Anyone with a grudge?'

'Not that I'm aware of.'

'Were you in the graveyard for a while, or attacked immediately you went in?'

'Time is hard to estimate when you're a little drunk. I wasn't attacked immediately, anyway. I'd found one of the graves I was searching for and I was wandering around, looking for the other.

Jesus!' she exclaimed with sudden disgust. 'How stupid can you get!'

'Look,' McCadden advised. 'It's better if you don't slip into feeling responsible for the assault. What you did has no more necessary connection with being attacked than getting out of bed yesterday morning. If you'd stayed in bed, you wouldn't have been assaulted.'

'But when you said about the prowler . . . Have there been other attacks in the area?'

'No. There's a possibility – no more than that, as I said – that someone around has an unpleasant interest in celebrities. If there is, he must think he's in heaven since Hollywood rolled into town.'

'We're finishing here on Friday.'

'So I've heard.'

'What should I do?'

'I'm sure your security people will be hemming you in from now on. You'll have to put up with it for a few days. We'll continue the investigation. I'll probably need you to show someone exactly where you were attacked. If it's any consolation, I don't think it's a personalized attack. So it's unlikely you're in continuing danger.'

'It leaves a bad taste, though,' she said sadly. 'I thought I was still more or less ordinary around here. Now I can't relax . . . '

ten

Outside, Paul Hyland was waiting for McCadden.

Camped in the centre of the car park, surrounded by admirers, Hyland seemed to be entertaining a gadget-laden special effects crew with robotic impressions of the local characters. Even on a film set, he managed to reflect the sunlight.

Breaking away from the group, he walked to meet McCadden, lighting a cigarette along the way. He looked well, McCadden had to admit. Lightweight summer suit, tan leather shoes, a couple of sparkling pieces of expensive jewellery.

'Nice number you've got here,' McCadden complimented when they met.

Hyland took the approval in his stride. 'It's all about money these days, Carl, isn't it? The old values are gone. You have to go with the flow. I've got my own security firm. It's where the future is. Look after your own business by getting a professional to look after it.'

The last two years, four senior officers above the rank of superintendent had left the force for the same lucrative rewards in the private sector. McCadden wasn't in a position to argue the toss.

He asked, 'So who have you got in the frame for the assault on Cathy Morrison?'

Hyland smiled, rocked his left hand back and forth to indicate a teasing uncertainty, and took a devious route. 'Heard you got very cosy with her yesterday.'

'I'm a fan, Paul.'

This time, Hyland's smile bordered on the lecherous. 'Aren't we all? Did she say anything negative about anyone in particular?'

'Have you talked to her?'

'Not about the assault. She wouldn't discuss that. Insisted on whispering for your ear only. But my job is to know things, head off trouble before it hits.'

'Not this time, though,' McCadden scored.

Hyland tried to shrug it off, but was irritated. His polish never *had* got anywhere much against McCadden's coolness and the failure still grated slightly. He said, 'My five against your one says the guy you're looking for is Michael Constant.'

'I still don't gamble, Paul.'

'You play the odds, just like everyone else.'

'Why Constant?'

'Recent form. His girlfriend, the handicapped one, has been trying to make contact with Cathy Morrison. He resents it. He's a possessive little fucker. She's a domestic pet to him. Short leash, daily walk, couple of tricks and don't crap on the living-room carpet. A couple of days ago he was down here threatening retribution if we didn't return her to him. He'd lost her somewhere. But it wasn't here. This is only the icing, though. His real gripe isn't with Cathy Morrison. It's with Bill McMullan.'

'Why?'

'There's a history there, Carl. A little side show to the titanic clash between peasant Ireland and the Celtic Tiger.'

'Paul . . . '

'Don't knock it. Listen to me. Michael's mother was the Widow Constant. Have you heard of her?'

'A little.'

'She lived in the same cottage he's in now, when there were only four, five houses on the entire headland. She was famous, man. A healer. A herbalist. A witch, some said. People travelled for miles around with all the ailments of the old days. Rickets. Rheumatism. Tuberculosis. Bad luck. Now, people just take tablets. That ring a bell? Tablets? Pharmaceuticals? Lisenter? Bill

64

McMullan? It's the kind of weird connection the crazy little man makes. His mother died about ten years ago. There's still some mystery surrounding the death. Maybe suicide. Not to the white-haired boy, though. He *knows* the multinational rubbed her out. Here we are, a couple of months from a new millennium, and we're still screwed up by superstition. Look at those fucking nuts out there, for instance.'

'Have you got any evidence to link Michael Constant with the assault, Paul?' McCadden wondered.

'You going to talk to him?'

'Probably.'

'Tell him to lay off hassling Mr McMullan, will you? If he's got a beef, put it on the table where we can all judge it.'

'I think you'd better tell him that yourself. And have Mr McMullan's lawyer with you when you do.'

'I don't mean it literally, Carl. Just a quiet hint. Like the old days.'

'Except the old values are gone.'

'You know something? The only thing I really miss about leaving the force is the company, the slagging, the camaraderie . . . '

McCadden's attention drifted, softened by the false nostalgia. Looking out beyond the barriers at the entrance to the car park, he rehearsed what he had to say to the rival groups still picketing outside.

He was going to need the names of all those who'd been in the pub the previous night, along with the movements of anyone who happened to be on the roads or around the graveyard, apart from the old man who'd responded to Cathy Morrison's moans and found her semi-conscious. He didn't anticipate problems with co-operation. The local community was too eager to keep the film company on side.

The eco warriors offered a different challenge. They'd prob-ably be tempted to infiltrate along the flanks of the car park and occupy the sand dunes when darkness fell, trashing in the process some of the habitat they'd come to protect from the ravages of Hollywood. Maybe a warning that they were suspects in a serious case might hold them off. Maybe not. Either way, he'd want to know when each of them arrived, where they'd slept, whether they had records.

He looked finally at Sergeant Mullaney. The big man had positioned himself significantly, facing down the eco warriors, with his back to the local protesters, making it clear where he imagined the source of any treachery was.

The sergeant should really be taking statements from the witnesses, doing the bulk of the legwork in the case. But McCadden thought again of the look of bruising lust on his rough face when they'd been standing outside Eleanor Shiels's bedroom window a couple of nights before. He didn't trust Mullaney. Certainly not with women. Not because the man desired them. Sexual excitement was fine. Natural. So was voyeurism, really. But police work was *public* work. And a cop should have the discipline to maintain an acceptable public face.

He'd send someone out from the detectives' office in Waterford to take charge, McCadden decided. Rose Donnelly, probably. As a bonus, Rose's take on Sergeant Mullaney, and on Paul Hyland, would be interesting . . .

eleven

Driving away from the film set, McCadden stopped at the top of the lane. On the opposite side of the main road, about fifty metres to his right, was Michael Constant's bungalow. The site of the stone cottage with the half-door featured in the photograph that accompanied the clipping her son had preserved, McCadden realized now. Like most of the others on the headland, the original dwelling had been razed and built over in contemporary style.

It was easier to demolish buildings than memories, though. Because obviously, the old woman was still a presence on the headland.

Despite his interest, McCadden had already decided not to call on Michael Constant. Or not today, anyway. He knew that the man hadn't assaulted Cathy Morrison. Constant was too small. It was as simple as that. He couldn't have comfortably reached her mouth with his left hand if they were standing on the same level. And even if he'd stretched that far, he couldn't simultaneously have laughed in her ear. Cathy Morrison was about the same height as Ellen O'Doherty. And Constant had to strain to eyeball his girlfriend, even when she stooped.

What concerned McCadden more was Paul Hyland's eagerness to push the little man forward as a prime suspect. Hyland wasn't offering any evidence. He hadn't even checked the basic facts. He was just blatantly inviting collusion.

Presumably, Hyland was working to Bill McMullan's agenda. Was there some ongoing dispute between Constant and the businessman? Some residue from the past? Was Constant currently pressing a lawsuit, for instance? He was certainly the type for litigation. A self-styled protector. Of dead and living women. Persistent. Single-minded. Slightly paranoid. And goaded by a chafing sense of grievance.

Teasing it out, McCadden turned left as he accelerated out of the lane, drove on past the graveyard, and took the next right back into Waterford.

He didn't bother reporting at the station when he reached the city. Nothing there except untended paperwork. A sleepy desk sergeant. A couple of early drunks or brawlers in the cells. An empty detectives' room. And besides, he was anxious to check his answering machine at home.

There was only one message waiting for him, though. And it wasn't the one he'd hoped for.

Carl? It's Roberta again. Are you away? Didn't you get my message on Monday?

McCadden cursed. Roberta Gavin. Stand-up comic. Last seen in Waterford doing a pub gig about three years ago, when she got so entangled in a murder investigation that she was in the frame as a suspect for a while.

She was the colourful date McCadden could've had on Monday night, if he hadn't spent the time chasing down those shifting images of Eleanor Shiels and the shadow of Rookie Wallace. He'd forgotten about her in the meantime and never returned her call.

The machine instantly offered forgiveness, though.

Anyway, it said, *I'm back in Waterford tonight. Wednesday night? Not a gig. I'm talking to some people. I'll be in Geoff's bar from about eight-thirty onwards . . .*

McCadden looked at his watch. Almost eight. Plenty of time to shower, shave, change his clothes and summon a taxi.

But he didn't move.

He knew that he wouldn't have made even passable company that night. He was too uneasy. Too preoccupied. Oppressed by the kind of moody dedication to the job that used to convince his ex-wife that he wasn't ready to father a child, until she also convinced herself that he wasn't ready to be a husband either and divorced him.

Except that he couldn't understand its source now.

Was it that fleeting glimpse of Rookie Wallace in Waterford? His doubts about Paul Hyland's motives? Or something more personal? The need to prove himself, to publicly demonstrate his talents, in the run-in to the appointment of the head of the new Murder Squad, a position McCadden wanted so desperately that he was aware of his own desire as a weakness, leading him into temptation.

The trouble was, his job was routine at the moment.

Apart from the assault on Cathy Morrison, admittedly. Was that supposed to be a test for him? Were the minister and the commissioner monitoring his handling of such a sensitive problem? Was everything riding on that?

Because otherwise, the work was dull. Clerical. Within the range of an average pen-pusher. No murder. No major case. Nothing except his own vague concern, his nagging ignorance, about Rookie Wallace and Wallace's interest in Eleanor Shiels.

It was what he was really staying at home for tonight, he realized. The expected phone call. Illuminating that darkness. Filling him in on Wallace's current status and form.

He could've diverted incoming calls to his mobile, of course, and headed out anyway. But the pub wasn't the best place to wait on bad news. And he always found it easier to keep a vigil alone.

It was what separated the gregarious from the loners, he felt. Whether or not they wanted company when they were under pressure. He didn't.

He erased the message on the answering machine and headed for the kitchen to make some coffee.

twelve

Early next morning McCadden despatched Rose Donnelly to take charge of the investigation in Brownstown, having squared the arrangement with Sergeant Mullaney and established that there'd been no overnight raiding parties of eco warriors, no pitched battles between locals and outsiders.

For the moment, things seemed to have stalled in the country.

Held up again for medical treatment to Cathy Morrison, the film crew hadn't resumed shooting yet on the set of *Sacrifice*. And maybe that had been enough to satisfy the warriors' short-term ambitions.

Elsewhere, McCadden made gradual progress.

He interviewed the doctor who'd treated Cathy Morrison in Casualty. As McCadden suspected, her wound was almost certainly caused by a fall rather than a blow. Probably against a headstone, the doctor suggested. A slab. A stone memorial of some sort in the cemetery.

The chances were, whoever had grabbed her, presumably with sexual intent, had released her again almost as quickly, before he'd had time for a sexual assault. And he'd dropped her carelessly, out of necessity. Already limp and unconscious, she'd fallen heavily against a monument.

The interruption could hardly have been anything as minor or unthreatening as someone walking past the graveyard on the road. His reaction wouldn't have been as sudden, as extreme. The attacker would've continued holding his victim, making sure she stayed quiet enough and still enough not to raise the alarm. Or else, if he knew she was already unconscious, he would've put her *gently* down, not risking waking her while preparing his own silent escape. Instead he'd just abandoned her. As if he'd been surprised himself. As if he had to defend himself.

But if the rescuer was *that* close, McCadden wondered, why hadn't they discovered the victim under their feet? Or if they had, why hadn't they immediately summoned help? Were they already known to each other, the attacker and the witness? Was one eager to cover for the other? Were they two members of the same group, for instance, sharing objectives, but with conflicting methods? The wise and foolish eco warriors, perhaps?

Either way, McCadden was now more confident of an early break. *Someone* had disturbed Cathy Morrison's attacker. At least two people, other than the victim, had been in the grave-yard. And that more than doubled the chances of a lead.

After that, of course, it depended on how vigorously the brass wanted to push things along. Would they bring the same forensic investigation to bear on the case as in a murder, say, analysing fibres, bloodstains, DNA? How many officers would the Chief Superintendent authorize? The more you put on the ground, the quicker you got more reliable results. Or was this just a cosmetic exercise, as false as Bill McMullan's bronzed and surgically ravaged body?

You should never underestimate the depths of official cyn-icism, McCadden reminded himself. For the moment, an impressive investigation, headed by an inspector, was good PR. But the film company would withdraw to a new location in a couple of days. The eco warriors would all go back to occupying the woods of County Wicklow. And unless there was a serial sex offender in the area who struck again, the assault on Cathy Morrison would go down as the handiwork of some obsessive fan on a one-off curve.

Driving back to the station from the Regional Hospital, McCadden's mood was uncertain, despite the progress he'd made. Still shot through with the uneasiness from the previous night, it was now darkened a little more by the black political border around the Morrison case. Politics worked to a different agenda from law enforcement. Politics was all about popularity, acceptability, image. And it was about as helpful at a crime scene as a fat egocentric child demanding exclusive attention after wandering away from its doting mother.

But politics would also determine who was appointed head of the Murder Squad.

As it turned out, McCadden's vague apprehension was quickly justified.

Within a minute of sitting at his desk, he learned from three different sources that the Chief Superintendent had left urgent messages for McCadden to contact him as soon as he showed up. The key to reading the bite in the instruction was that phrase, *showed up*. Loosely translated, it revealed the Chief Superintendent's exasperation at McCadden's trifling with minor interests when something vital was over-cooking back at the office.

McCadden dragged the phone towards him and buzzed through. And amazingly, Cody seemed thrown by the call. He stuttered and then said coldly, 'Give me, ah, ten minutes. I'll see you in my office then. Ten minutes.'

This tension between the old man's burning desire to gaze on McCadden and his ability to defer his own satisfaction was a little more disconcerting. McCadden moodily watched the clock. When it struck eleven, not quite ten minutes later, he wandered off, climbed the stairs and pushed straight into the Chief Superintendent's office after a light knock.

He knew immediately that there was trouble ahead.

Two visitors were already sitting inside with Cody. And there was no other chair left in the room for McCadden.

So the ten-minute pause requested by Cody had been put to creative use, summoning this pair and precisely arranging the mood and parameters of the interview that was to follow.

McCadden instantly rebelled. He went back out, snatched up a plastic chair from the corridor and carried it into the office.

'We seem to be short,' he explained drily.

He wedged the chair between the two visitors, forcing them apart. When he sat down, he'd already changed the composition of the group and the nature of the meeting. Now there were three of them facing the Chief Superintendent, instead of three confronting himself. And the two outsiders could no longer stare at him without also looking at each other.

McCadden already knew the visiting pair. Knew them both as sad, unpleasant bastards. Although they were slightly different *breeds* of the same species.

The guy on his left was a zealot. In a hard, religious, unforgiving sort of way that McCadden had seen so many times before in so many others. The same soulless eyes and thin, dry lips. The same starved flesh. The same shrivelled heart that was fed exclusively on sacrifice, of himself and of others. And the same cold feel, reminiscent of a headstone in a graveyard, that the righteous always had.

The character on the right was a foot soldier. A country lad. He shared the same values and standards as his mate, but he'd never managed to get quite comfortable with the icy exterior. Wasn't the type. As an expression of his rustic warmth, for instance, his clothes were rough and untidy. His frayed black pants and dull check jacket contrasted with the sharp grey suit of his friend, just as his slack unshaven face was the opposite of the other's ascetic thinness and pale features.

Tom Reynolds and Jerry O'Dea. Tom and Jerry. Not yet as famous or as casually violent as the original partnership. But working on it.

McCadden wondered what calculating shyster had sent the pair down to Waterford. And on what mischievous errand. By himself, O'Dea – the homely countryman – was unimportant. But Reynolds was dangerous. A high-profile Special Branch inspector. Ambitious. And probably McCadden's closest rival for the Murder Squad job.

Cody looked uneasy as he made the introductions. While he talked, he sought the comfort of his leather gloves. But he no longer had the composure to stroke them as usual and picked at them anxiously instead, risking damage to the stitching. 'This is, ah, Detective Inspector Thomas Reynolds and, ah, Detective Sergeant . . . O'Dowd?'

'O'Dea, sir.'

Not knowing what the source of Cody's embarrassment was, McCadden was reluctant to dig him out. He waited. When the Chief Superintendent had finished, he turned to Reynolds and asked innocently, 'You down here on holidays, Inspector?'

Reynolds gave a thin, watery smile that did something slightly uncomfortable to his lips. 'I don't think so.'

'You don't *think* so?'

'Business.'

'Do you *take* holidays?'

The smile died on Reynolds's lips. He took a small notebook from the inside pocket of his jacket and flipped it open. He said, 'You made a telephone call, Inspector—'

'Where are *you* going, Jerry?' McCadden switched suddenly.

O'Dea clearly had a contribution to make. And he was clearly rehearsing that contribution. But he wasn't expecting his cue for a while yet. He jumped and looked appealingly past McCadden, towards his master. 'What?'

'On your holidays,' McCadden clarified. 'Where are you going this year?'

'You made a telephone call, Inspector,' Reynolds cut in again. 'Last Friday. To Kevin Street Garda Station in Dublin. Do you remember the content of that call?'

This was a hostile interrogation, McCadden suddenly realized. The first time, apart from training exercises, he'd been on the wrong side of one. First time he'd played it for real. First time he had to absorb and process new information while struggling to keep the exchanges going and not revealing too much with his silences.

He knew now, for instance, and *only* now, why his call to Dublin about Rookie Wallace hadn't been returned, even though the query had been a confidence shared with a trusted friend. His call had been monitored. His friend had been duped, somehow diverted into believing that the information was being conveyed to McCadden by other means.

But for the moment, that was all McCadden knew. He had no idea what this pair of cut-throats from Special Branch were actually looking for. No idea of what was prompting their questions.

He said, 'Its content? You tell me.'

Reynolds didn't react. 'My query is part of an official invest-igation, Inspector,' he said smoothly. 'By not co-operating, you risk being charged with obstruction.'

'Oh, dear,' McCadden sighed ironically. 'Obstruction.'

'Precisely.'

'Investigation into what?'

'Would you please answer my question?'

'Tell me,' McCadden invited. 'How many official calls did I make to Kevin Street last Friday?'

'One.'

'Wrong.'

'How many?'

'None.'

Reynolds's lips stretched themselves painfully again. 'I'm afraid that's untrue.'

'Look,' McCadden offered, 'I'll give you the benefit of the doubt. I'll assume you know the difference between official and unofficial, between formal and casual.'

'Now you're taking refuge in semantics.'

'Maybe my trust in you is misplaced. Maybe you *don't* understand the difference. I don't know. I'll risk it, anyway. You claim you're running an *official* investigation here. You have an odd way of going about it. If you want to know something about this district, use the standard procedures. You can go about it the casual way or you can go about it the formal way ... Personally, I don't much care about the style. But if you know something that impinges on policing in this area, share it with us. Otherwise don't bother me.'

Reynolds exchanged a look with Cody.

McCadden might've been wrong, seeing only half the exchange, but he reckoned it was a *vindicated* look, a look confirming some suspicion they'd previously shared.

'Last Friday', Reynolds said then, 'you contacted Detective Inspector Christopher Smith, who works at Kevin Street Garda Station, and you asked him to run a check for you on a man named Tony Wallace, also known as Rookie Wallace.'

'Go on,' McCadden encouraged.

'Why are you interested in Rookie Wallace at this particular time?'

'I know him.'

'I'm aware that you know him.'

'Then you're also aware why I'm interested in him.'

'But why *this* particular time?'

'It's been so long since I saw him. He came into my head. Not for the first time this year.'

'What put him into your head?'

'Previously?'

'This time.'

'I don't mean to be flippant, but I think it would take someone with more expertise in the odd workings of the brain than either of us to make a decent stab at that one.'

'When was the last time you saw Wallace?'

McCadden thought. Long enough to indicate a quick, unworried search through the memory files. Not so long as to suggest doubt or anxiety. 'Two years, I think. He was pulled in for questioning in Dublin. I happened to be around.'

'Have you seen Wallace lately?'

'Does two years qualify as lately?'

'Within the last month.'

'No.'

'Have you had any indication that he may be in Waterford?'

'In Waterford? No. He would've contacted me, I think.'

'You haven't seen him in Waterford?'

'Are you saying he *is* in Waterford?'

'I'm asking you.'

'I'd find it surprising.'

Reynolds made a dry, economical gesture, lifting dust from the armrest of his chair when his hand settled again. 'Thank you, Inspector. That's all I need to know.'

McCadden nodded. 'Right.'

And for a while, the silence crackled with suppressed menace.

Until the Chief Superintendent cleared his parched throat. 'Have you, ah, anything else you need to ask?'

Reynolds didn't respond, allowing space at last for O'Dea to make his contribution. 'No, sir. That's grand, now.'

'Good, good . . . '

It was obvious that Cody was lost. He was floundering a little, starting to flail with his arms and legs. Just *beginning* to be gripped by fear. All of which could only mean that Reynolds carried unseen weight into this contest, that he was probably a messenger boy from the commissioner or the Minister for Justice. And Cody still had too much of the old-fashioned reverence for authority to go up against that.

McCadden looked at the old man with his usual mix of pity and slight contempt and knew that he could expect no help from that corner. The Chief Superintendent had already abandoned him, already turned away in terror from the pack.

McCadden tried to think then of something to confuse or hurt Reynolds. But he couldn't.

He had no idea what was going on, no idea whether his outrageous lie about seeing Rookie Wallace had damaged his credibility or wriggled him off a fatal hook.

He was blind. Wounded. Aware that he was losing. So goaded by unseen blows that for a moment he was uncharacteristically overwhelmed by a paranoid fantasy. Maybe it was all a plot, he thought wildly. Wallace, the Minister, Reynolds . . . A plot to get him smelling so badly of shit that the interview board would just turn away from him in disgust.

It sounded improbable. But it was also possible. Rookie Wallace, for instance, had claimed to know Eleanor Shiels. She claimed never to have heard of him.

Floundering in the dark, but too proud to show it, McCadden stood up. He swung a finger towards O'Dea. 'I'd recommend Dunmore East, Jerry.'

An easier target, O'Dea was immediately knocked off balance again. 'What?'

'For your holidays. You'd enjoy Dunmore East. You're a fishing man, aren't you?'

'No, I—'

'Maybe you'll put the chair back out in the corridor, Jerry. If you don't need it for someone else.'

McCadden left without even scattering a few courtesies. His

77

only mistake, he reckoned later. His only admission that he'd been bruised.

He took a detour on his way back to his office, boiled a kettle of water in the canteen kitchen, made a cup of Rombouts coffee and carried it with him. When he sat down at his desk, he gave his full attention to savouring the coffee for a few minutes. Then he set to work.

On a blank foolscap page, he scribbled crowded notes in neat little columns. It was something he did whenever he was totally at sea. The apparent order on the paper compensated for the messy confusions of reality. Didn't alleviate them, of course. Just replaced them for a while.

Within the columns, he worked with dates. Days. Weekends. Calendar months. Another artificial structure. Time on paper was always somehow consoling.

From Monday, 24 July, to Friday, 11 August, he noted, he had been away on holiday.

Not a great holiday . . .

But that was a separate worry. And a minor one now.

On Friday, 11 August, he had returned to Waterford. Among other messages on his home answering machine, there was one from Rookie Wallace, dating all the way back to Friday, 28 July. A lengthy message, reminding him of old times, lamenting the unacceptable gap since they'd last seen each other, and asking him if he could manage to scrape together some background on the former rock star Eleanor Shiels, who was now living in seclusion out on Brownstown Head.

That same Friday, McCadden had contacted Kevin Street Garda Station in Dublin and asked Detective Inspector Chris Smith to run a confidential check for him on Rookie Wallace. But even though Smith had promised quick results, McCadden hadn't heard from him all weekend.

Monday morning, McCadden tried Kevin Street again. Inspector Smith wasn't available. Why not? The woman on the switch didn't seem to know. Maybe he was away on holidays, she said. Maybe his wife was giving birth. Maybe he'd been floored by a stomach virus. Had he left any messages for a DI Carl McCadden? No . . .

McCadden rang Smith's home number. No one there to pick up the phone. A standard message on the answering service. *Not available at the moment . . . leave your name and number . . . we'll get back to you . . .*

That Monday night, dulled after a day playing catch-up with the paperwork that had accumulated during his holidays, McCadden had driven out to Brownstown Head and called on Eleanor Shiels.

Eleanor Shiels . . .

He was just finished neatly writing her name in the fifth column on his foolscap page when his telephone rang. Irritated, he looked up at the receiver's display. The call was from the front desk.

He jabbed the button. Shouted into the speaker. 'Yeah?'

'There's a lady at the desk requesting to see you, sir.'

'Will you take her name, Sergeant? The nature of her business. I'm in conference right now.'

He closed off and went back to his pretty, uninformative patterns on the page.

Thirty seconds later, his phone buzzed again. The same button illuminated on the pad. Front desk.

He pressed it with a pen. Angry now. 'What is it?'

'Sir? The lady who's looking for you. She says you'll want to see her, sir. She says her name is Eleanor Shiels . . . '

thirteen

She was wearing a plain white T-shirt, faded navy jeans, tan belt and shoes, and wraparound reflective shades that were lifted off her face and resting on the peak of the white baseball cap covering her head. Her long black hair was flowing from under the rim of the cap, across her shoulders and over her back.

Forty-four years old, but still distracting a couple of wide-eyed rookies from their duties. Kids just out of training college the last few weeks, whose anxious mothers were probably younger than Eleanor Shiels herself.

And her mood had changed with the outfit, McCadden immediately noticed. She'd dropped both the haughty distance of the previous Monday night, when he'd been slightly wrong-footed after blundering into her cottage, and the cool detachment she'd shown at the funeral of Artie Logan the following morning. She was more alluring now. Trimming her appeal with a touch of vulnerability to attract the male, with the sense of a slightly bewildered woman stranded in alien territory and surrounded by hard-nosed, military men.

Her pose was too polished, McCadden guessed, and too self-conscious, not to be a preparation for something else. And her first words confirmed his suspicions.

She glanced at the watch on her left wrist and asked, 'You don't *have* to interview me here at the station, do you?'

He shook his head. 'I don't have to interview you anywhere.'

'Could we go somewhere else in that case? I think I might need lunch.'

McCadden had no objection. For the moment, Reynolds and O'Dea were polluting the pond at home and the further he got away from them the cleaner he felt.

'If you don't mind walking,' he said. 'It's not very far.'

Outside, the midday sun was intense. The dry spell that had started during Artie Logan's funeral on Tuesday was now turning itself into an official heatwave. The footpaths felt hot, even through the soles of McCadden's heavy shoes. To the right of the station, there were noisy roadworks. A pneumatic drill was jabbing into the ground and turning over clumps of disintegrating concrete. But in front of the steps some of the recently laid tar was already softening again with the heat, forming slow bubbles in the cracks it was supposed to seal.

McCadden and Eleanor Shiels turned left and walked down Patrick Street, too awkward with each other for casual conversation and moving too quickly for serious discussion.

The traffic was light. Traditionally, August was a holiday month in Waterford. In the old days the population had crowded the nearby seaside resorts, keeping within a radius of fifteen or twenty kilometres from home, as if still attached by a cord. Now they jetted to Spain, to Crete, to Barbados ... The result was much the same. Apart from the tourists sucked inwards by the lure of Waterford Glass and the Viking towers, the city was half-deserted in August. And its better restaurants, preparing local produce, were mostly empty.

'What do you reckon?' McCadden wondered as they reached the junction of Broad Street and Patrick Street and waited at the lights. 'Health food? Chinese? Indian? Italian?'

'Maybe a pub?' Eleanor Shiels suggested.

'A pub?'

'I don't think I'm really that hungry.'

'But you said—'

'More thirsty than anything.'

'Right.'

'Do you know Egans?'

'Yeah, fine.'

They turned left again, into Barronstrand Street. Inside Egans – one of those old-fashioned pubs from the mid-nineteenth century whose wood and stone interior offered the illusion of escape from commerce – they found a cool, darkened corner. McCadden, still on duty, settled for a coffee and a ham and salad roll. Eleanor Shiels drank Guinness.

When she toasted him, she observed mischievously, 'You look tense, Inspector.'

He shrugged, made a half-hearted stab at flirting. 'Well, it isn't the company, anyway.'

'What is it? The job? It can't be a very satisfying occupation for anyone intelligent.'

'As much as it always was.'

'I don't believe that. I don't think you do, either.'

'Well, I try not to say things I don't really believe in. Maybe I'm out of touch.'

'When I was a girl, Inspector, a policeman was respected, maybe a little feared. Now you're just derided, aren't you? Pug-faced kids on poor estates. Trendy liberals. Anyone in the media. The only people who love you are insurance companies.'

'It's happened to all forms of authority in Ireland the last decade. It's not necessarily a bad thing.'

'Public indifference on one side. Sleaze from your political masters on the other. Graft. Corruption. Did you hear the news this morning? Your Minister for Justice is sailing close to the wind again. A forty-thousand pound campaign donation in a plain brown envelope? Jesus! And no record of any of it ever reaching party funds? How will he wriggle out of this one? But he will, won't he? He's not dumb enough to be poor, or underprivileged, or unable to afford a lawyer.'

McCadden ate his bread roll, using it as an excuse for not answering. He was already annoyed by his choice of lunch. The crusty roll took so long to chew that his coffee cooled. And if he drank the coffee while it was still hot, the liquid made the bread soggy in his mouth.

But he knew that he wasn't in the humour for being pleased by anything. Sore and resentful, he also knew that he was susceptible to a woman's sympathy and concern. He needed to keep his mouth shut as much as possible.

Eleanor Shiels took off the white baseball cap and placed it on the table. She punched a little well in its crown and nestled her sunglasses inside. As she looked back up and considered McCadden, she tilted her head to one side. Her long black hair fell across her face. She left it there, peering at him from around it.

'You're not going to ask me, are you,' she said.

'What?' he muttered stubbornly.

'Why I wanted to see you.'

He swallowed the food in his mouth, put the remains of the roll on the plate, dabbed at his lips with the paper napkin. 'I figure you'll tell me when you want to.'

'Are you a patient man, Inspector?'

The query invited intimacy, a shift in their relationship from the professional to the personal, the brisk to the languid.

'Depends on the worth of what I'm waiting for, I suppose,' he hedged. 'And you?'

She laughed and threw her head back. Ran the fingers of her right hand through her hair to brush it away from her forehead and left her palm, with the fingers entwined in the hair, resting on top of her head while she answered. 'I come from *the* impatient generation, Inspector. Restlessness was a way of life with us. When you tired of eating hamburgers, you could just order pizza next time. When you tired of your parents, you could have your own kids instead. And if the Children of Divine Light didn't immediately bless you with spiritual harmony, you could always try transcendental meditation, or paganism, or acid the next weekend.'

'Why did you quit your career as a singer? Restlessness, too?'

Her hand dropped from her head. And with it her body sagged a little, indicating disappointment. 'Is that what you find most interesting about me?'

McCadden took the spoon from the saucer, idly stirred the coffee in his cup. 'In my experience, most people make small decisions all the time. It's the accumulation of small choices that makes up their lives, their attitudes. It's very rare to find such a sudden shift, particularly when lack of talent isn't the cause. So, yes, at the moment, anyway, I find this the most interesting thing about you.'

'You're very direct, aren't you?'

'Something that comes with your awareness that time is running out.'

'What does that mean?'

McCadden shrugged and tapped the face of his wristwatch with a finger.

Eleanor Shiels slowly shook her head at him, not accepting such an obvious evasion. 'When I was *young*', she said, 'I was into directness, too. I was interested in politics. And protest was the political gesture of the young at the time. Nineteen sixty-eight, through to the early seventies. I thought music was a form of political expression.'

'Wasn't it?'

'No.'

'Another of the period's clichés bites the dust.'

'Not rock, anyway. In public, it was just an obscene gesture for effect. *Fuck you!* Two fingers to the old establishment. In private, it was all about money and consumption. Swiss bank accounts, corporate decisions, fast cars, fast women, fast drugs. Just capitalism with a street-cred image.'

McCadden had finished his food. He looked dubiously at the unappealing cold coffee and wondered if he should give in to the temptation to order some booze, ease into an afternoon of reminiscence, regret, nostalgia. He said, 'That was an impressive analysis for – what? – a nineteen, twenty-year-old?'

She laughed again. And at herself again. 'No. That was just the way I rationalized it all years later. I really got out of the business because I was scared. I couldn't handle it any more. I got lost. I looked in the mirror one shitty morning and it suddenly hit me that I was feeding my career by killing myself. It was the only fucking way a woman could make it big, be really famous back then. By selling herself as a victim. That's what excited the public. Maybe now still. You look at some of the stars now ... The way I did it, I played up my nightmare background. My alcoholic father. My depressed mother. My abused childhood.'

'*Sexually* abused?'

'What other type is worth commercializing?'

'I'm sorry ... '

'And Jesus! Did it sell! Did it go down a bomb! Did it put everything in context for the fans and the media! The booze. The drugs. I was *their* captive as well, just like I was Daddy's captive as a girl. That's how the fans understood me. The running away from home to gig in London suddenly made sense of running away from the gigs themselves, from making commitments. The pain of the old abuse suddenly made sense of the new pain of self-abuse. The tabloids loved to splash my pain on the front pages. At first, it was done with sympathy. Then it was critical. By the end, it was just disgusted. They build you up to slap you down again. Suffering makes people irritated once the initial sympathy is exhausted. Once they've parted with a charitable buck, once they've paid for their ticket to the Live Aid concert or pledged their donation to the Telethon, they want you to get out of their sight again. But I didn't cop that. I couldn't let go. I got entangled in the image they created of me.'

'"My Old Man Shot Me With A Camera",' McCadden remembered.

Eleanor Shiels sat back. She brushed the hair from her face again, showing a look of mild astonishment, wide brown eyes and slightly parted lips. 'I still have fans, do I?' she asked.

'Closer to home than you might think.'

'Oh?'

'Michael Constant?'

But she dodged unexpectedly. So quickly and smoothly that he couldn't tell whether it was intentional or not. 'I heard that you wanted to interview Michael Constant in connection with the assault on that young actress. Isn't that the phrase you use? *In connection with?*'

'Helping with enquiries.'

'That's it! *A thirty-eight-year-old vertically challenged male is helping the Gardaí with their enquiries . . .*'

'Where did you hear that I wanted to talk to Michael Constant?'

'I have my sources on the headland.'

'Sources? I've spoken to only one person on the topic.'

'Oh,' she smiled, 'my contacts go much higher than the mere head of security for the film company.'

And McCadden was suddenly struggling. And had to admit it. 'You seem to be a couple of steps ahead of me.'

'More than a couple, Inspector,' she claimed. She finished her drink, immediately catching a barman's eye to order another. When she turned back towards McCadden, she said, 'Michael Constant was with me in my cottage on Tuesday night. I know that the assault on the actress took place between eleven and one. Michael was with me at that time.'

McCadden stared at her. His only slight advantage, he decided, depended on not revealing that he already knew that Constant wasn't involved in the attack, in letting the investigation flow as normal and seeing where it took them. He asked, 'Are there any other witnesses?'

'Don't you trust me, Inspector?'

'Is Michael Constant a friend of yours?'

She grimaced at the fuzziness of the term. 'Friend? Our relationship is a little odder than that, I think. Have you seen his display of press cuttings?'

'Yes.'

'He told me you had.'

The barman served her a fresh pint of Guinness, took her payment and the empty glass from the table. She watched him retreating and only turned back to McCadden when he was out of earshot again.

'There's nothing really scary about Michael, you know,' she said. 'He's pretty harmless. He has a weakness for failures, that's all.'

'In what way?'

'Faded icons. While the rest of the world is dazzled by the latest stars, he wants to resurrect the forgotten celebrity. It makes him feel important. And out of sync at the same time. It's weird. But it's not threatening.'

'What about your next-door neighbour? Mr Newburn?'

'Sonny?'

'Would he be able to verify Michael Constant's visit to your house on Tuesday night?'

She frowned, looked at him with a little less artifice. There was a trace of something negative in her eyes now. Resentment.

Doubt. 'I suppose he could,' she said, 'if he wanted to. But I guarantee that he'll swear he was listening to Bach all night with his eyes closed and the curtains drawn. Seeing no evil, you know. And not hearing anyone on the road outside.'

'Why would he do that?'

'Michael is not very popular on the headland.'

'Because of his mother?'

'Partly. She certainly scared a lot of people when she was in her prime. A lot who were children then claim they still have nightmares about her. She was supposed to have the power to put a curse on you. But these are more enlightened days, aren't they? So the prejudice against Michael has as much to do with finance as it has with superstition. Michael agitates against Bill McMullan's pharmaceutical plant in the area. He's very dogged. Very persistent. Very much a thorn in their side. But it's not a popular campaign. The local economy now depends on the plant. It's been allowed to squeeze out everything else. And no one really cares about anything except prosperity any more, do they? All the locals ever talk about is their salaries, the price of their properties, the capacity of their bloody car engines.'

'Why does Constant persist?'

'Why do you think?'

'I assumed it was his mother. But you're clearly suggesting that there's something else.'

His tone, slightly fractious now, seemed to make her wary, worried that she might've added too much playfulness to the mix. She bowed her head slightly and said softly, 'You're right. There is something else. It's because of Ellen O'Doherty, actually.'

'The young woman he's living with?'

'Specifically, because of the cause of her illness.'

'What about it?'

But just as he closed in, she slipped maddeningly sideways again, suddenly running on a parallel track before he could reach her. 'How well do you know Bill McMullan, Inspector?'

McCadden sighed, but held his patience. 'I met him for the first time on Tuesday.'

'And Artie Logan?'

'I never met him. I know nothing about him. Apart from the fact that he grew up in Boston with McMullan.'

Eleanor Shiels offered a sad, ironic smile. 'Oh, they both grew up in Boston,' she accepted. 'But not on the same side of the tracks. Artie was drafted and sent to fight the war in Vietnam. He got decorated, but he came back disillusioned and joined the civil rights movement. McMullan was a ward politician in South Boston, fighting for the endangered rights of the white, Irish Catholic working class, as he put it himself. But he really distinguished himself when the courts ruled in the mid-seventies that Boston's schools had to be desegregated, that the races had to be mixed. He organized pickets, boycotts, harassment. He even has a conviction for assaulting a black teenager who was being bussed to school.'

McCadden frowned, letting his doubts surface. 'What's the source of this information?'

'Don't you believe it?'

'He seems an unlikely ally for an Irish government Minister to keep on his arm.'

'Oh, that was a quarter of a century ago,' she said airily. 'The taint has faded away now, just like my own fame, and McMullan has cleaned up his public act in the meantime. Well, he's stuffed the nastiness out of sight, anyway. People are very adaptable, Inspector. What seemed like racism back then was really only patriotism, you know. And ruthlessness is only the flip side of sentimentality. I'm sure you've heard that I became friendly with Artie Logan since he came to work here?'

'It's been mentioned.'

'When he came to trust me, when he saw that I was on the same side of the political fence as himself, he told me about an interesting sequence. *Interesting* is not the right word. Sickening, perhaps. Lisenter – Bill McMullan's company – once had a pharmaceutical plant in Edinburgh, Scotland. When it pulled out, it left behind a redundant workforce, and a young woman named Jennie McMordie, who'd been healthy when the plant was established and was now so severely brain damaged that she was a mere vegetable. In Boston, as a young man, McMullan dated a young Catholic girl named Bridget Sullivan. Bridget died at twenty-one. The story was, she committed suicide.'

'And Ellen O'Doherty?' McCadden asked.

She looked up at him, held the stare for a moment. 'Ellen O'Doherty was working for Lisenter as a temporary, vacational staff member when she was brain damaged.'

McCadden felt a cold, hollow sensation in his stomach. He also felt a little queasy, as if the ham roll was going to be rejected by his gut. He needed a vodka to warm him now. But he didn't want to expose his discomfort. He said, 'Didn't she fall from a cliff during a works outing?'

'You didn't know that she was working for Lisenter, did you?' Eleanor Shiels asked.

He shook his head. 'No, I didn't.'

'So you haven't yet checked the details of the case?'

'No.'

'Check them. It says she fell while rock climbing in the Comeragh Mountains, that her two companions were male friends she made at Lisenter, and that there were no other witnesses. There are discrepancies. Michael Constant was the only one to pick up on them afterwards, just as he was the only one to care for Ellen.'

'Are you suggesting that the fall never happened?' McCadden asked bluntly.

'I'm quite certain it didn't.'

'*What* happened, then?'

'I suppose you've come across every oddity in the course of your work, Inspector. Men with perverse sexual desires, for instance. Men who choke themselves while masturbating, so that the lack of oxygen will heighten the sensation. Men who get their kicks from choking others. Men who prefer the unrespons-iveness of a warm corpse to a demanding, living woman. It's probably old hat to you by now, is it? Not to me. I've made it my business to get to know Bill McMullan since he arrived in Ireland a few weeks ago. We now have a *curious* relationship. What I've always enjoyed, is playing men's lust against their self-interest. It's not something you'll find analysed in the tabloids, but this is what I always fell back on, even at my lowest. *Especially* at my lowest. Woman as victim? Woman as bait? I'm very good at it. But men are also *very* stupid. Their self-interest invariably limps in a poor second. Bill McMullan, for instance, hates what I stand for, but he desires me. Above all, he desires me naked and bound. It's what turns him on. Handcuffs. Thongs. Straps. Halters. Submission. Dominance turns him on. Last Monday night, when you called at my cottage, I was waiting for him. My front door was open to welcome Bill McMullan. The cottage was in darkness because that's how he likes to work. I was waiting for him in my bedroom.'

Reeling a little, caught between repulsion and allure, between the thought of McMullan's plastic surgery mechanically imposing itself on a woman and the image of a yielding Eleanor Shiels, her black hair spread across white sheets, McCadden could only find a stock, absurd question. 'Why haven't you reported all this before?'

'You're a senior police officer, Inspector,' she reminded him. 'Would you move against Bill McMullan without hard evidence? Considering his standing with the local community? Considering his political connections? I don't have any evidence. I don't have any powerful friends in high places. All I have is a dodgy plan to offer myself as bait in a trap for him.'

A barman came and took the remains of McCadden's coffee, the now empty pint glass. He placed them on the counter and returned with a cloth to clean the table. He lingered at it, probably hoping for another order. But McCadden's appetite, even for booze, had long since died. And Eleanor Shiels seemed to share his mood.

When the barman was gone, McCadden leaned forward, his elbows on the table. He said, 'I asked you on Monday night if you knew a man named Rookie Wallace.'

She shook her head. 'I don't know anyone named Rookie Wallace. Is he a policeman?'

'Why does that occur to you?'

'If he's interested in me, it strikes me as a possibility. More of a possibility than a stalker or a prowler. Since Artie's disappearance, since they discovered his body, I've been more cautious, more suspicious. Artie's death ... that, too, went down as an accident.'

'You don't think it was?'

She laughed, emptily. 'No, I don't believe I do, somehow.'

McCadden sat back again, considering her silently for a moment. He said quietly then, 'You didn't trust me on Monday night, Ms Shiels. You were almost obstructive. Today you seek me out and you're open. What made you change your mind?'

She looked across at him, her dark brown eyes alive with confidence again, and slightly amused. 'I discovered that Bill McMullan dislikes you intensely, Inspector,' she said. 'More than that. More important than that. He's actually *scared* of you. Scared enough to get your own superiors to cramp your style. I don't know the precise reasons, obviously, but that in itself is a good enough recommendation for me. And after Artie ... I've got to trust someone, haven't I? Someone more capable than Michael Constant. You're going for promotion at the moment, aren't you? McMullan told me that. He laughs about it, says he has your Minister for justice in his pocket, and even though you have the best qualifications, you have about as much chance of landing the job as a snowball has in hell. His own unseasonable cliché, I'm afraid ... '

fourteen

The sunlight hurt McCadden's eyes when he left the darkened interior of the pub and stepped on to the crowded footpath outside. He tapped his pockets, looking for his sunglasses, but then remembered that he hadn't taken them from the car before walking down Patrick Street with Eleanor Shiels. He was forced to wait until his eyes adapted, stranded on the footpath and squinting uncomfortably. The situation struck him as comic. A blind detective, he thought, searching for a reliable hound to guide him.

Except the joke was a little too close to the bone to fully appreciate.

Walking slowly back to the station afterwards, along Barron-strand Street and up the hill to Ballybricken, he teased out what Eleanor Shiels had just confided.

What bothered him, although he hadn't mentioned it to her, was why such opposites as Bill McMullan and Artie Logan were so eager to hop into bed together.

He could understand *one* side of that deal.

Accept that McMullan was a dangerous sexual predator, he proposed to himself. Accept that he squeezed some twisted kicks from tying up women. Accept that it occasionally went off the rails for him and some exploited kid ended up with brain damage after being starved of oxygen.

This was what Eleanor Shiels was claiming. This was what she claimed that Logan had revealed to her.

Accept all that. And that Logan had decided to infiltrate

McMullan's operation and thereby get close enough to the perv to trap him in the act. That was fine. A bit unorthodox, tinged with improbable romantic heroism, like a Hollywood movie, but plausible enough, if you accepted the premise.

But why the hell had *McMullan* employed *Logan*?

McMullan had nothing to gain from the arrangement. Why bring a troublemaker on to himself? A political radical, if Eleanor Shiels's description was accurate. An aggressive crusader. And why fly him all the way across the Atlantic to sit on the very doorstep where McMullan had just dumped his own shit?

Blackmail? But if Logan had enough dirt on McMullan to pull that one off, then he didn't need to go sneaking around searching for dusty skeletons. He could've come straight out and put the charges on the table.

It didn't add up, McCadden decided. It just didn't balance. Or not yet, anyway.

Back at the station, he sought out Frank Ryan for an update on local news and heard that Reynolds and O'Dea had slipped out to lunch with the Chief Superintendent.

'I wonder who's paying,' he muttered.

Ryan anxiously searched his bitten fingers for remnants of nail to chew on. 'What's up, Carl?' he worried.

McCadden shook his head. 'I'm not sure. I'm kind of groping around in the dark at the moment. Who was dealing with the Artie Logan file, Frank?'

'Jerry Tobin. He started holidays on Monday.'

'Logan's body was found last Thursday. That right?'

'Uh-huh.'

'When did he go missing, do you know?'

Ryan puffed air between his lips, as if the effort was physical as well as mental. 'About a week before that. I can check the date.'

'Will you get in touch with the American Embassy in Dublin as well? One of their Marines was at Logan's funeral. I want to know when and where Logan served in their armed forces. I want to know what the protocol is, whether they have a colour party at every ex-serviceman's funeral. Ask them about his post-service record also, if he was an anti-war agitator at any stage. Who did the autopsy on Logan, by the way?'

'Hugh Craig came down from Dublin. Straight in and straight out. No complications. I don't think he left any option for the coroner, other than bringing in a verdict of accidental death.'

'Right. A couple of other things. This is spreading the net fairly wide, so I've no idea how we're going to do. Better take a note of these. See if Lisenter, McMullan's pharmaceutical company, had a plant in Edinburgh, Scotland, and if a Jennie McMordie ever suffered an accident while working there. See if you can discover if Bill McMullan has a criminal record in Boston, probably dating back to the early or mid-seventies.'

'Jesus!' Ryan exclaimed. 'That's going to stir some shit. Just *asking*'s going stir the shit.'

'I know, I know. Use my name, not your own. And keep this stuff away from Tom and Jerry, obviously. Actually, keep it just to yourself, Frank. I'm going out to Brownstown for the afternoon. Rose Donnelly's already out there. Give her a buzz, will you? Tell her to meet me at the entrance to the film set out there in an hour and a half.'

McCadden left the station a little after two-thirty.

He drove first to the fishing port of Dunmore East and from there followed the odd route that Artie Logan's funeral had taken the previous Tuesday, partly to search for clues to the man's crowded life and lonely death in the obscure locations where the cortège had stopped, partly to call at the Lisenter plant, a kilometre short of the graveyard at Corbally, which the funeral procession had passed without reference to on the day.

He gained nothing from the first part of the journey and was losing patience with the stunning coastline by the time he reached the pharmaceutical plant. Sitting outside its entrance, waiting for the barrier to be raised, he noticed irritably that the security guard on the main gate was from Paul Hyland's company. And when he drove inside, yet another of Hyland's employees directed him to a parking space, clipped a visitor's badge on his lapel, and escorted him through revolving glass doors to the building's lobby.

The young woman behind the reception desk, a straw blonde with a blur of light-brown freckles, looked nervous when she saw his ID.

'Oh, that'll be Mr Parks,' she said when McCadden asked for the boss. 'Mr Parks is our assistant managing director. Our *former* managing director was . . . '

'Yes, I know. Arthur Logan.'

'But Mr Parks is in conference right now.'

'It's urgent,' McCadden growled.

He sat on a brown leather couch and waited, watching the traffic go by. The whole company, he noticed, seemed to be infected with a kind of wary anxiety. Tense tea ladies. Jumpy security staff. Uneasy secretaries. He wondered if it was one of the side-effects of the drugs they manufactured.

Even Parks himself, a balding little man with shrivelled features and the alert eyes of a frightened animal, was so edgy that he jumped the gun after the introductions. 'Is this about Mr Logan?' he asked.

'Why would it be about Mr Logan?' McCadden wondered.

'Well, his unfortunate accident . . . '

A bearded man in a white coat, looking too obviously evil, like a mad scientist in a B-movie, drifted furtively past, lingering by the drinks machine in an effort to overhear.

'Maybe your office is free,' McCadden suggested.

'Of course, of course . . . '

It turned out to be a dead man's room. For some reason, they hadn't yet removed the old nameplate from the door of what used to be Artie Logan's den.

'It was easier to move myself to the mountain of files,' Parks hurriedly explained. 'Rather than, you understand, attempt to move the mountain . . . '

'Right.'

'Would you like tea, coffee, anything . . . ?'

McCadden shook his head. 'Thanks, but I don't really have time. Do you have a personnel officer here?'

'I deal with company employees. At least until we appoint a replacement for . . . '

'Good,' McCadden muttered.

It was necessary, he'd decided, to keep tossing in meaningless sounds to bring one exchange to an end and encourage the advance to the next. Parks was one of those characters who never seemed to finish a sentence. Perhaps the full stop had too much finality for him. Perhaps he liked to leave those gaps for adjustments, alterations, reversals ... Definitely not a natural decision-maker, in any case.

McCadden said, 'I'm interested in a young woman named Ellen O'Doherty. I believe she worked here last year. Do you remember her?'

Parks blinked rapidly a couple of times. 'Yes, yes ... ' He sat behind his desk, leaving McCadden still standing, and fidgeted with a framed snapshot of a harsh-looking middle-aged woman who might've been either his mother or his wife. 'Very sad. It was all ... was all *regularized* with the insurance company, you understand, and ... '

'I'm sure it was,' McCadden accepted. 'I'm not interested in that area.'

'Aren't you?'

'I'm really enquiring about the young woman's background. Can you remember how long she worked here?'

'Well, it all sticks in the mind, doesn't it, when something like that happens. It was over the summer. Purely a temporary thing, you understand.'

'What did she work at?'

'I believe she was an actress, professionally.'

'I mean, here.'

'She covered a number of areas while employees were on holidays. Receptionist, clerk ... '

'Office work?'

'Yes.'

'Did she have any involvement in the manufacturing process? Did she handle pharmaceuticals?'

'No. Could I ask ... ?'

'Was Mr McMullan forced to come over from America to deal with the tragedy? Or did Mr Logan handle it?'

'Mr McMullan? Mr McMullan was already in the country at the time.'

'Yeah?'

'I'm sure all this is in your files, Inspector. Mr McMullan was negotiating finance and locations for his film, *Sacrifice*. Miss O'Doherty was an actress. Did I say that? She was quite confident of landing a major part in the film and . . . '

'Right. Is Mr McMullan here at the moment?'

'No. He's on the set of the film.' He indicated the telephone on his desk with a nervous little movement of his right hand. 'Shall I . . . ?'

'Better not,' McCadden advised. 'They're not going to like a mobile phone suddenly ringing if they're shooting.'

He offered a handshake, knowing that the little man would be breathing down the line as soon as he was gone, dutifully tipping off his boss.

Parks stood to accept the handshake. 'As regards Miss O'Doherty,' he said tentatively. 'Is there some . . . ?'

McCadden raised an eyebrow. 'Some?'

'Some . . . '

'No,' McCadden said decisively. 'Definitely not.'

fifteen

A couple of kilometres away, down at the entrance to the film set, Rose Donnelly was already waiting for McCadden. She was sitting on the bonnet of her parked Corolla, with her legs swinging loosely, coolly studying an edgy security guard, who was on the other side of the barrier blocking off the car park.

There wasn't much else to hold her interest in the area.

The eco protest had faded as quickly as it had formed and had now thinned to just a pair of stalwarts. The two were still dressed in paramilitary gear. Obviously suffering as much from the heat as from disillusionment, they were slowly and silently describing a diminishing circle as they picketed. But they were too clearly beaten, and too sad, to attract a counter-picket any more.

Perhaps the young protesters, like most of their generation, were actually movie buffs, McCadden thought, uneasy about the politics of disrupting a shoot. Perhaps, like everyone else, they hadn't been able to decide whether film was art or commerce. Or perhaps the local opposition was just too heavy and too consistent for them to sustain the illusion that they'd come as saviours.

Rose Donnelly slipped from the bonnet of her own car and walked across to sit in the front passenger of McCadden's after he'd pulled up. Without waiting for the query, she flipped open a notebook she took from her pocket.

'OK,' she said. 'My *guess* is that it's not one of the locals. They're all so outraged they would've thrown us the bastard by now if they knew who it was. I've interviewed everyone who was in the pub on Tuesday night. I didn't have to search for them. They all came forward. Cathy Morrison left the premises a couple of minutes either side of eleven-thirty. She left alone. No one followed her. There were a lot of guys who might've been interested in making a play for her, but they were all watching one another.'

McCadden indicated the tiring picketers through the wind-screen. 'What about the eco warriors?'

'Most of them left this morning.'

'On the run?'

'No. I think they split because of a row within the group. I talked to them before they left. They all arrived together in a convoy early Wednesday morning, six hours after the attack. It puts them out of the picture.'

'Which leaves the film company itself,' McCadden accepted. 'Or some other outsider.'

'Apart from Cathy Morrison, I haven't interviewed the film's cast and crew yet. I talked to the local staff in the hotels where they're staying, but not to themselves.'

'And the scene?'

'I had a look. It's right at the back of the graveyard, well away from the church and the road. She hit the side of her face on one of those low stone enclosures around an old grave. She had slight abrasions to her hands and bare legs, caused by granite chips from another plot she was standing on. The odd thing is, she wasn't otherwise damaged. It seems like someone grabbed her and just let her go again as soon as she fainted.'

'She mentioned that her clothes were in disarray.'

'Probably only from the fall. What I'm saying is, her clothes weren't loosened or removed. And the medical report is definite that there were no contusions other than the ones caused by the fall. Unless we've got a freak who just enjoys looking at helpless women in sexually available postures.'

Revising his earlier suspicion that two of the eco warriors were involved and shifting his thoughts again to the world of the movies, McCadden drummed his fingers on the steering wheel and muttered, 'Funny you should say that, Rose.'

Donnelly stared at him. '*Is* there a freak, sir?'

McCadden ruefully shook his head. 'More likely that someone disturbed the attacker,' he admitted. He gestured again through the windscreen, indicating the unreal world beyond the barrier this time. 'How are we doing with the beautiful people?' he asked. 'Have you got access organized?'

Donnelly nodded, leaning away from him to put the notebook back in her pocket. 'There's a production assistant waiting to give us the guided tour. Are we going?'

'Wouldn't miss it,' McCadden enthused. 'The way the film industry is abandoning Ireland these days, the opportunity might never come again.'

The production assistant was an energetic young woman with long brown hair who seemed to do everything at about double the necessary pace. She talked so rapidly that there was always a time lag between the end of one of her sentences and her listeners' uptake, a gap she insisted on filling quickly with even more words. McCadden was still shaking her hand in greeting while she'd hurried beyond the outline of their schedule for the visit and had them back at the starting point again, ready to leave.

'Right,' he struggled.

As she led them away, through the car park, down to the beach and past the local authority signpost that told them they were approaching a bird sanctuary, she kept scurrying too far ahead of them, realizing they'd lost contact and dropping contritely back, only to quickly shoot off again. Because of her movements, her voice drifted in and out of range, like a weak radio signal, full of fuzzy vowels and screeching emphases.

'... don't know at *all* why *anyone* should be worried,' they heard her claim. 'There's a wildlife officer actually *monitoring* the situation. And we're not *using* the habitat itself. The Burrow is just background. You *see*! They're working on the *beach* ... '

They *were* on the beach, McCadden confirmed. Although working was surely the wrong verb. There were about a hundred people in the area, but they all seemed to be standing around, just waiting.

The production assistant suddenly stopped, glanced back, and waited impatiently for the two detectives to reach her out-stretched arm. 'They've actually started *shooting* now,' she whispered. 'We have to be still and *quiet* until the director has finished. The *director* is the man . . . '

Even from a distance, the tension on the set was obvious. A sense of desperation. Of time as pressure and work as a burden.

Two figures, Cathy Morrison and her leading man, both dressed in costumes from the fifties, met in front of the massive dunes. Unable to hear the dialogue, McCadden struggled to understand what they were doing, reviving memories of agonized encounters with the mime artists his ex-wife used to drag him to watch in Dublin theatres. They might've been sparring, he thought facetiously. Or playing a children's game. Although neither seemed very likely.

Whatever they were supposed to be doing, they weren't doing it very well. The director suddenly jumped to his feet and sliced through the quietness with a sharp, irritated voice. 'Cut! CUT!'

The command was echoed by a score of fawning assistants who immediately squirmed into life around him. 'CUT! CUT!'

'Let's take a break, *everybody*,' the director wearily called in a martyred tone that suggested there was going to be no such deliverance for himself. 'God knows, we all need it. Martin! Where are you, Martin?'

The production assistant instantly lowered her outstretched arm. 'Now!' she shouted. As if they'd been toeing the starting line, had just got the off and her arm was the starting gate. Within ten paces she was already too far ahead to discover where the detectives wanted to go or who they wanted to see.

McCadden watched her being swallowed by a swarm of extras. When she'd disappeared, he indicated a direction to Rose Donnelly, across to where Cathy Morrison and her co-star were standing, surrounded by fussing make-up artists, fastidious dressers and dialogue coaches . . . All of whom should surely be on a coffee break. Or had McCadden got it wrong? Was the director the only one who had earned the right to put his feet up?

'Who *is* that guy, Rose?' McCadden whispered.

'Who, sir?'

'The mannequin. The actor. With Cathy Morrison.'

'Him? That's Hank Panusi.'

'Who?'

'He played the psychiatrist's house-help in the television comedy series *The Jung Generation*. Do you remember? It tried to jump on the success of the *Frasier* bandwagon. And he was one of the cops in the show SPUC. It was supposed to be an acronym for *Special Police Unit Command*, but it got confused over here with the anti-abortion lobby, Society for the Protection of the Unborn Child, and had to be dropped from the schedules.'

'How do you know these things, Rose?'

'My little girl watches them.'

'Right.'

By then the discussion between Morrison and Panusi was so loud, and so animated, that it was obvious they were no longer trying to act.

'For Christ's sake, Cathy, you've got to give me a *break* here!' Panusi was pleading. In his carefully torn shirt and rolled-up trouser legs, with his bronzed flesh and rippling biceps, he looked, McCadden thought, more like a gay Californian body builder than an Irish agricultural worker of the fifties. And his falsetto voice did nothing to challenge the image. 'I've got to feel as if I'm *losing* something here!' he squawked.

Cathy Morrison was simmering with repressed anger. She seemed about to explode and perhaps fatally damage the working relationship with a few home truths, but instead raised her eyebrows and spread her lips in a thin, strained smile of welcome as the two detectives approached.

Just for the fun of it, McCadden decided to pitch in on her side. 'Are you supposed to be *Irish*?' he asked Panusi innocently.

The actor bristled. 'What kind of goddamn question *is* that?' he demanded.

'He's a detective,' Cathy Morrison grinned. 'He asks those kind of questions all the time.'

McCadden indicated the entire enterprise with a sweep of his hand, the actors and technicians, the cameramen and caterers, all scurrying about on the most industrious coffee break he'd ever witnessed in his life, hoping he was getting a look of awed admiration on his face. 'What's this film about, anyway?'

Panusi, obviously uncomfortable with anything wider than the close-up, was immediately thrown. 'Well . . . ' he struggled.

'Ms Morrison cautiously directed me to your publicity department the last time I asked.'

Panusi snapped gleefully at the bait. 'Oh, no, it's no great secret. I can't *believe* Cathy was that coy. It's really *the* Irish theme of the summer, you know.'

'Like bright T-shirts with pale-coloured suits?'

'No, no . . . '

Bob Bettesworth, the film's director, suddenly broke into the group with a nervous, darting movement that seemed to be his style. He clearly had urgent business on his mind. But his leading players had separate agendas. And more vital irritants.

'Will you *please* talk to this man about my character, Bob!' Cathy Morrison pleaded. 'He wants me to throw it up to him like a fucking hooker!'

'The detective was wondering', Panusi put in simultaneously, 'what our film was about.'

Bettesworth was already slightly dazed. 'Film?' he repeated.

'Its theme,' Panusi explained. 'Its subject matter.'

'Yes! Quite!'

'Bob!' Cathy Morrison summoned.

'Yes, darling.'

'Specifically,' Panusi persisted, 'its relevance to modern Ireland.'

'She's a *country* girl,' Morrison pointed out. 'Growing up in an insular society. She's sexually inexperienced.'

'I've been *trying*', Panusi stressed, 'to explain it to him.'

Bettesworth was lost. 'I'm sorry, Hank?'

'The movie's *theme*, Bob?

'Oh, right. Yes. Ah . . . Inspector McCadden, isn't it?'

McCadden nodded. 'This is Detective Donnelly.'

'How do you do. Yes. Well, ah, the film is really about unresolved tensions within the central character at a period of great change, for himself and his society, in the late nineteen-fifties. The opposites are represented by his parents. His father is a police sergeant . . . '

'A *police* sergeant?'

'Yes . . . '

'What an extraordinary coincidence.'

' . . . gregarious, pragmatic, welcoming the expansion of horizons in the new Ireland of the time . . . '

'Well, he would, I suppose.'

'But his weakness is booze . . . '

'Of course.'

' . . . which coarsens his personality. The mother is a woman of great serenity, great learning and understanding . . . '

'The standard Irish matriarch.'

' . . . but for all her spirituality, there is about her a vague sense of unfulfilment.'

'And the girlfriend?'

'Well, the character's tragedy is that he aspires towards the spiritual world of his mother, but always seems to end up living in the rougher world of his father.'

'So the girlfriend suffers.'

'I'm afraid so.'

Like watchful chaperons, others had now been sucked in by McCadden's presence and by his obvious curiosity. Bill McMullan came and stood at his director's shoulder in the middle of the synopsis, making the Englishman increasingly edgy. Paul Hyland planted himself beside his boss a little later, his arms folded and his legs spread, holding a tough, uncompromising posture.

Bettesworth, prompted by his producer, the most unforgiving of all timekeepers, breathing down his neck, glanced at his watch, looked upwards at the declining sun, and then reached sideways in both directions to draw his feuding stars towards him. 'Would you excuse us?' he requested. 'We really *do* have to get back to work.'

'Could I just detain you a moment longer?' McCadden asked. 'Now that you're all here. It won't take long.'

They looked at him warily. And his central role, with so many expectant eyes on him, made him a little uneasy at first.

'Detective Donnelly and myself,' he explained, 'in the course of investigating the attack on Ms Morrison, have been taking statements from potential witnesses. We've already covered the local community and now need to interview employees of the film company. We thought it might be a good example to others if we started at the top. Mr McMullan. Mr Bettesworth. Mr Panusi. That sort of thing. We're interested in your movements on Tuesday night last, between eleven p.m. and one a.m.'

Bettesworth was first in, because he wanted to be first away again. 'It's quite straightforward in my case,' he said. 'I was studying the day's rushes with my editors. It's something we do every night.'

'Mr McMullan?'

'Got to admit it, I was whacked Tuesday night, Inspector. Hate to say it, but I spent the evening and the night in my hotel bedroom after a short drink at the bar.'

'Mr Panusi?'

Panusi had been frowning. 'I'm not too sure, I guess.'

'You had a drink with us, Hank,' McMullan volunteered. 'Remember? We shared the end of the Jim Beam.'

'Yeah, I guess. I mean, I hadn't thought about it, is all. Maybe I can get back to you, Inspector?'

'Well, Detective Donnelly will be staying to complete the statements . . . '

When the group had broken up, with Bettesworth dragging his stars away to patch up their rift, McMullan clicked smoothly into the role of expansive host, with only the occasional sharpness in his glittering eyes to remind McCadden of Eleanor Shiels's warning.

'You ever been on a film set before, Ms Donnelly? First I had the pleasure of was *Five Easy Pieces*, way back in sixty-nine . . . '

He led them to the front of the gallery, within a pace or two of the director's chair, and kept name-dropping amiably until the crew were ready to reshoot the scene.

Up close and able to hear the exchanges, McCadden at last

understood the nature of the encounter between the characters played by Morrison and Panusi. Like most mysteries, its exposition was banal. Although there were freakish echoes of real life that were disturbing.

The man wanted sex. And the girl didn't. In the hope of both pleasing him and capturing him in the pleasure, the girl finally yielded. Disgusted by her fall from grace, the man rejected her. A blow expressed his rejection. A blow that gradually turned into a vicious assault and descended into rape, despite the girl's earlier submission.

Throughout it all, McCadden kept a sly watch on Bill McMullan. Because the glossy old man seemed in thrall himself, vividly living the experience of one or other of the characters, his absorption either ignorant of, or enhanced by, the unsettling fact that Cathy Morrison was recreating her real-life trauma.

When it was all finished, when the director was out of his chair announcing it was a wrap and there was general relief on the set, McCadden, feeling slightly tainted by what he had witnessed, quickly said his goodbyes and wandered back with Rose Donnelly and Paul Hyland, along the beach, up the stone steps into the car park, and towards the exit.

At the barrier, with Hyland still in tow, Donnelly asked quietly, 'Could I see you in your car for a minute, sir?'

McCadden was surprised, but tried not to show it. 'Sure.'

Hyland flashed his brilliant teeth in a predatory smile. 'I'll wait for you, Rose.'

Donnelly grimaced. Hyland had already made a play for her, McCadden remembered. A few years back, before he'd resigned from the force, and before he'd separated from his wife. Donnelly obviously hadn't softened her distaste.

Sitting in the front of McCadden's Mondeo, she took the notebook again from her pocket. 'It's Mr McMullan's statement that he spent all Tuesday night in the hotel, sir,' she explained. 'It doesn't tally with what I already have. According to one of the night staff, Mr McMullan came in the rear door of the hotel, through the grounds, a little after two o'clock that night. His clothes were muddy. He seems to be under the impression that he wasn't seen.'

'Great,' McCadden sighed.

'Do I face him with it, sir?'

McCadden shook his head, waving amiably through the windscreen at the patiently waiting Hyland beyond the barrier. 'No,' he said slowly, drawing the syllable out while he thought, trying to disentangle the disparate threads that were getting knotted here. His own personal feelings. McMullan's political agenda. His own ambition. The Special Branch sniffers still back at the station. He said, 'Without actually mentioning it, Rose, without drawing attention to it, see if you can build up a picture of McMullan's movements that evening and that night.'

sixteen

By seven that evening, McCadden had a written report from Rose Donnelly, confirming her suspicions.

Bill McMullan had returned to the hotel after the end of the day's shooting on Tuesday. He'd shared a couple of drinks at the bar with Hank Panusi and a few other actors. Twice or three times he'd asked where Cathy Morrison had got to, before retiring early to his bedroom at about ten-thirty. Nobody had seen him after that, until the night porter, enjoying a furtive cigarette in the gardens, had caught him sneaking back with dirtied clothes a little after two in the morning.

McCadden, hoping to relax by catching a film at the local screen, changed his mind after the contact from Rose Donnelly and put in a frustrated evening at home instead.

It was the worst of situations for him. A failing of his that always irritated him. Off-duty, unable to advance a case, but even *more* incapable of letting it go, he tended to mull over the thing obsessively. Couldn't take any pleasure from reading. Couldn't even watch TV. And certainly didn't want any company.

After drifting restlessly around the flat for hours, he finally fell asleep at one, still frustrated by his own ignorance. Woken again less than an hour later by some drunks on the street below his window murdering a Jennifer Lopez number, he just about resisted the temptation to get up and make some coffee. He seemed to hear the phone ringing as he slipped back towards sleep. He struggled to keep himself awake and was relieved, when he dragged himself back into consciousness, to hear that it was still ringing. But the digital clock, he noticed, now said six forty-two.

Baffled, he picked up the receiver and mumbled into it with a clogged voice; 'Yeah?'

'Carl? It's Frank Ryan.'

McCadden was bewildered. 'Is it Scotland?' he guessed.

'What?'

'I asked you to check on Lisenter and Bill McMullan in Scotland.'

'No ... I mean, that's in train, but there's no news yet. And I'd hardly pass it on at six-thirty in the morning, would I? Listen, you better get yourself dressed, Carl.'

'Are you in work, Frank?'

'No, I'm in the car, on my way to collect you. I'm about two minutes away from you now. Get dressed, will you? I'll wait for you outside.'

Tired after a broken, restless night, slightly disoriented now, and with the beginnings of a headache jabbing at his tensed neck muscles, McCadden still didn't question the arrangements. Ryan was too experienced, and too reliable, to make a call like that without reason.

It was already bright outside. The night had been warm and the morning was going to be hot and cloudless again. With no idea where they were heading, McCadden decided that chinos and a light shirt were probably safest.

After dressing, he hurried downstairs from the open loft and into the kitchen to brew some coffee. The car horn sounded from outside just as he was pouring from the jug. Grabbing a leather jacket, he took the mug with him, tasting the coffee on his way down the interior stairs to the front doorway.

Ryan was sitting outside in one of the station's fleet, a two-litre Hyundai Sonata. He seemed to get a kick out of handling it on the empty streets. Almost before McCadden had settled into the front passenger seat, he was pulling away, into a noisy U-turn, speeding back along Manor Street and then swinging left, heading for the shortest route out of the city to Brownstown Head.

'Jack Redmond's the night-duty sergeant,' he explained. 'I had a bad feeling yesterday, after we talked, so I asked him to give me a buzz if anything came up.'

'Right,' McCadden accepted. 'So what came up?'

'We have a body. Almost definitely a murder victim. You know the Saleens?'

McCadden's interest scrambled up a notch. The Saleens was an isolated beach about a kilometre east of Brownstown, between the head itself and the fishing port of Dunmore, and close to Lisenter's pharmaceutical plant. 'Yeah, I know it.'

'A couple of English guys have been camping out there on a touring, fishing holiday. They were going to cast off from the beach this morning to take the early tide when they found the body washed up, with what looked like stab wounds all over it. Might be the rocks, of course.'

'OK. But what's the panic, Frank? Are the fish going to come and take it away again?'

Ryan jauntily swung the car as he dodged pot-holes on the main road through the housing estate of John's Park and then accelerated into the country. He gave a low, hollow laugh to indicate that he'd heard the quip, but didn't think much of it. He said, 'Redmond had to ring the Chief Superintendent. The Chief Superintendent immediately woke our two Special Branch guests. So Reynolds and O'Dea are on their way out to the Saleens as well. We've got to beat them there. Or hope de Burgh or Rose Donnelly get there first. I kicked the two of them out of bed, as well.'

McCadden massaged his stiff neck, looked out at the speeding hedgerows. 'Why are the Special Branch men interested?'

'Because they think the body is this character called Rookie Wallace they're so keen on.'

'How do you know about that, Frank?'

'About Wallace?'

'Uh-huh.'

'Reynolds and O'Dea spent the whole day asking around the station yesterday. *Everybody* knows about Wallace now. Without knowing anything about him.'

'Why do they think it's Wallace lying on the beach in the Saleens?'

'Because the corpse is from Dublin. He's wearing a Dublin hurling jersey.'

'Surely he—'

'No, I know what you're going to say. But this is an interesting thing, Carl. You find a guy wearing a Manchester United kit, or an Arsenal shirt, or Liverpool's, the chances are zero of him being from Manchester, or London, or Liverpool. I mean, even if he's one of the club's fucking *players*, the chances are slim. But that's the beauty of the GAA. Only Dubs would wear the Dublin jersey. Only Waterfordians would wear a Waterford jersey. And that's the way it should be. Don't you think?'

'No doubt.'

'So this Wallace guy. He's from Dublin, right?'

McCadden nodded. 'In a way.'

'You know him, don't you?'

Ryan wasn't prying. Or he wasn't *only* prying. He was wondering aloud if he could help a little more.

And besides, McCadden thought, the time had probably come to share a little of the burden. By taking this initiative, along with de Burgh and Rose Donnelly and others, Ryan risked making himself dangerously unpopular with the local command.

'Personally,' McCadden explained, 'I don't know him well. I've worked with him, but only for short periods. He covered my back once and I owe him the favour.'

Ryan frowned, took a quick glance across, even though they were hurtling along a narrow country road. 'Are you saying he's a member, Carl?'

'It wouldn't be safe for him to advertise that.'

'Even among friends?'

'He's been working undercover the last few years, mostly in the tougher Dublin estates. I don't just mean surveillance. I mean the whole hog. A new identity. No other home to go to at the end of the day. He's not from Dublin – not originally, anyway – so he's seen up there only as a drifter, a blow-in. He was born in Cork, I think. When I worked with him in Galway, he had a girlfriend he intended marrying, a good career ahead of him. The last three years he's been living off the dole, apparently. One kip after another in Dublin, with nothing but junkies and gougers for company. I don't know why he does it.'

'Something happen to the girlfriend?'

'I don't think so.'

'What was he like to work with?'

'I never really liked him, to be honest. It's why I never got to know him, I suppose. There was too much fervour about him, too much the man on a mission. Always had to be the best policeman in the world.'

'I know the type.'

'But he covered my back and I'm still in his debt.'

'What's he doing in Waterford?'

'I wish I knew the answer to that.'

'Looking for you?'

'I'm easy enough to find, Frank.'

'When did you last see him?'

'The day before yesterday, in Michael Street. I was driving. By the time I got out of the car, he'd given me the slip.'

'Doesn't sound like he's looking for you, does it?'

'He rang my home when I was away on holidays, towards the end of last month, asking me for information on Eleanor Shiels. You know her? The singer?'

'Living out here in Brownstown? Wasn't she interviewed after Logan's death?'

'That's her.'

'I'm beginning to see . . . '

'Wallace was calling in that favour, I suppose. But he hasn't contacted me since. Before all this, the last time I saw him was almost two years ago. You know Chris Smith in Dublin?'

'A little.'

'I was visiting Chris in Kevin Street in Dublin, hanging around the station waiting for him to wrap up something. They brought in a load of junkies and others in a swoop, and Wallace was among them. He saw me, but just ignored me. And that was the first inkling I had that he'd gone undercover. Nobody else there knew him and they just treated him like an ordinary suspect. I managed to get a few minutes with him in the interview room later and we caught up a little with each other. My impression was, Special Branch was controlling him. I'd reckon Reynolds and O'Dea are his current handlers.'

'So what are they saying? That's he's gone native? That he's bent?'

'They're not saying anything. Apart from the fact that they want to find him.'

'Which means they've lost contact with him. He missed his last appointment with his handler.'

'Seems like it.'

'How do they know he's in Waterford?'

'I don't think they're too certain, to be honest. I rang Chris Smith last Friday, asking him to check on Wallace for me, and they must've intercepted that, assumed that I'd met or seen Wallace down here. I haven't told them that I actually saw him the day before yesterday. They're still pretty much in the dark.'

'All the more reason for us to get to the Saleens first.'

'Looks like it . . . '

With his foot still heavy on the accelerator, Ryan swung left at Corbally crossroads, raced past Michael Constant's bungalow and took a left again. Ellen O'Doherty, McCadden noticed, was standing in the open doorway of the house in the same spot, and much the same posture, where Constant's mother had been photographed in a black shawl all those years ago.

She wasn't the only one disturbed by the early morning activity. Farmers watched from the gates of their fields as the car flew by, craning forward, their arms resting on the upper bars. And a couple of kids, restraining a barking sheepdog, pressed themselves back against the hedge, along the road's grass margin.

Five, six hundred metres down the side road, while preparing to accelerate out of a bend, Ryan hit the brake pedal instead and cursed softly. Ahead of them was a slow-moving Opel Omega. Jerry O'Dea was hunched over its steering wheel, Tom Reynolds was craning out of the open window of the door on its passenger side, and the two of them were searching desperately for landmarks and signposts, guides to the unfamiliar beach where a dead man lay waiting for them.

Ryan ran up close behind the Omega and leaned on the horn. But the Special Branch men only stared at him through their rear-view mirrors, refusing to pull over. And the road was too narrow to overtake.

Within a minute Liam de Burgh, travelling with a uniformed officer in a squad car, had tagged on behind, gesturing his frustration and his apologies at McCadden and Ryan. And the little convoy stayed in that formation, snaking along the country road, until it reached the Saleens.

They expected a scramble there, a frantic manoeuvring of cars, a jostling for advantage, even an undignified race to the corpse. But the entrance to the beach was already cordoned off with crime scene tape and Rose Donnelly, impressively dressed in a white boiler suit and surgical gloves, stood beyond it, guarding the pass.

Reynolds was the first to reach her. She blocked his path. Looking closely at his ID, she slowly studied the photograph, leisurely compared it with his face and handed the document back, all at the pace of someone whose brain was too sluggish even to *read* the examination paper for prospective Garda recruits. She didn't budge. And Reynolds, out of his jurisdiction and without written authority, could do nothing about it without risking a serious incident.

McCadden was only seconds behind. When he reached Reynolds, he slapped him consolingly on the shoulder. 'Sorry, Inspector,' he said cheerfully. 'Local problem. You'll have a copy of our report, of course.'

Reynolds angrily dipped his shoulder to slip away from the grip. He swivelled sharply and reached for the only available weapon. His mobile phone. His political connections. His influence with the brass.

McCadden left him to it. He asked de Burgh and the uniformed officer he'd travelled with to keep guard and then he stepped on to the beach with Ryan and Rose Donnelly.

To their left there was a green bell tent with its front flap open, home to the pair of sea anglers whose holiday had just been darkened. Ahead of them, straddling the line in the sand where the tide had filled before ebbing again, but with its back towards the approaching detectives, lay the sodden corpse.

From a distance, it might've been a drunk sleeping it off after a punishing binge. Apart from the outstretched left arm and right leg, the body was tucked into a foetal position, its bowed head almost cradled in its own limbs. As well as the sky-blue county hurling shirt, he was wearing a pair of torn jeans that were now too wet to determine their original colour and one white Nike Air trainer. His left foot was entirely bare.

McCadden already had his doubts – the Dublin hurling shirt had never really fitted with his expectations – but he kept his thoughts to himself until he'd walked around the body, forced wide by the crime tape preserving the immediate scene for the pathologist, and looked down at the dead man's face.

It wasn't Rookie Wallace.

It was a kid, really. Seventeen, maybe eighteen years old. Shaven head. A large silver medallion on a small ring dangling from the lobe of his right ear. A dragon tattoo on the biceps of his right arm. There was the impression of a wallet or a notebook in the front left-hand pocket of the jeans, where the material had been pressed against the skin with the weight of the water, but there was no way of retrieving or examining it until the pathologist had cleared the scene. The remaining sneaker, on his right foot, was loose around the ankle, but it seemed to be wedged against the foot by a cluster of small stones trapped inside.

It was obvious – to McCadden anyway – that the kid had died recently, no more than two or three days ago. There was no discoloration, no sign of swelling yet. But no *less* than two or three days, either, he decided. Rigor mortis had left the face and neck muscles, but seemed to be still present elsewhere, a combination consistent with a corpse being immersed in water for that period.

'Somebody mentioned knife wounds,' McCadden reminded the others, because he couldn't see any immediately.

'The throat is cut, sir,' Rose Donnelly supplied. 'It's concealed now, but the body was a little more open when it was first discovered.'

'Right. No chance of an accidental drowning, then.'

'No, sir.'

McCadden looked at his watch. It was almost eight o'clock. The state pathologist, even if he'd responded immediately to the summons, wouldn't arrive from Dublin for at least another hour.

But McCadden was reluctant to leave, even for a hurried breakfast or another coffee. Reynolds and O'Dea were still prowling, frustrated by their exclusion and probing for a weakness.

Twice – while McCadden was still considering the corpse – Reynolds dispatched a uniformed officer across the beach with a curt message, demanding to talk. Twice McCadden ignored the request. When he'd finished inspecting the body, he interviewed the two shaken anglers, then chatted to one of the local uniforms to get some idea of the tides in the area and only afterwards wandered across to Reynolds.

A small crowd had gathered by then at the entrance to the beach. No reporters yet. But they couldn't be far behind. Reynolds, wanting privacy to make his points, indicated the parked police cars. But McCadden stayed put, forcing the other into irritated, embarrassed whispering.

'Your Chief Superintendent has ordered you to allow access to the crime scene to myself and Detective Sergeant O'Dea,' Reynolds claimed.

'When was he here?' McCadden asked lightly. 'I missed him.'

'I've spoken to him twice on the telephone.'

McCadden glanced again at his watch. Still not eight-thirty in the morning. 'He must've been pleased.'

'As a direct instruction from a superior officer, the order must be complied—'

'Yeah, well,' McCadden interrupted, 'when I get the *direct* order from him I'll act on it. You'll appreciate that the usual procedures—'

'Have you identified the victim?'

'No, not *formally* identified,' McCadden teased, leaving the possibility that it *might* be Rookie Wallace still tantalizingly open.

116

Reynolds reached for him aggressively, but McCadden easily slipped away and went out of range again, back to the drying high-tide mark on the beach.

McCadden knew that he had breathing space. He knew that Cody was too wily, too much the cautious political animal, to put in an early appearance at the scene. The Chief Superintendent would keep his distance for the moment, avoid being tainted by the need to make executive decisions. He'd hold the kind of neutral balance that seemed instinctive to his rank, having done everything on the one hand to facilitate the visiting officers and nothing on the other to antagonize the local ones.

seventeen

It was past nine-thirty, and past McCadden's ability to keep himself even mildly occupied, when the assistant state pathologist, Dr Hugh Craig, finally turned up. McCadden had met him only once before. A tall, thin, crisply official young man. He was undoubtedly scrupulous, but since his precision also bordered on coldness, it was impossible to form an easy relationship with him.

Impressed by her spotless white boiler suit, Craig asked Rose Donnelly to assist him and the mortuary attendants with the preliminary examination. McCadden left them to it and only tried to prise a few opinions from the doctor when they were finally covering the body's head, feet and hands with plastic bags afterwards.

'How long?' he asked. 'Two, three days?'

'Two to four,' Craig drily corrected. 'I'll tell you more precisely when I've completed the post-mortem examination. But not *much* more precisely. Don't expect anything better than a guide to within twelve hours.'

'Was he dead before he entered the water?'

'I can't say for certain yet.'

'Likely?'

'It is *likely*, Inspector,' Craig said wearily, 'that the cause of death was the wound to the neck. Likely.'

McCadden sighed, wondering why the man had drifted into a job that needed an easy manner with both the living and the dead when he was obviously only comfortable with corpses. He gestured towards the body as they were about to cover and remove it. 'I need to examine the contents of the pockets. Can I do that now?'

'Not you,' Craig disapproved. 'Detective . . . '

'Donnelly, sir.'

It *had* been a wallet in the front left-hand pocket of the jeans. A cheap one, McCadden saw as Rose Donnelly tugged it out and flipped it open. Imitation leather. Badly torn and scuffed. Maybe *too* cheap for its contents. Inside, there were two hundred and fifty punts. Two fifties, six twenties and three tens. There was also a membership card for a video rental outlet, a doctor's appointment card and a provisional driving licence. All the documents had been issued to the same name. Vincent Woods, with an address on St Anthony's Estate in Dublin. And the passport-style photograph in the driving licence confirmed that Vinnie was indeed the corpse.

The zipped pockets around the rest of the jeans also yielded a couple of sodden, disintegrating packets of shag tobacco and cigarette papers and a small amount of cannabis resin in a waterproof bag. Otherwise there was nothing of interest. A few small coins. A cheap ring. A set of house keys.

McCadden had them all bagged and tagged, asked Frank Ryan to take charge of the final examination of the scene after the body was removed, and then accompanied the corpse as it was carried to the waiting ambulance, through the crowd that had now swelled with the spreading news.

This time he was questioned by reporters as he left. Absently trotting out the standard clichés, he noticed Eleanor Shiels and Bill McMullan on the edge of the crowd, apparently standing together. He nodded at them as he sat in the patrol car that had pulled up behind the ambulance. Eleanor Shiels responded with a slight smile and a gentle wave. McMullan, looking grimmer and greyer than usual, as if the plastic in his face had aged unexpectedly, didn't move at all.

McCadden didn't know the squad car driver, but quickly learned that he was relatively new to the force, that he was stationed in Dunmore East and that he already lived in dread of Sergeant Mullaney.

'Mullaney,' McCadden repeated softly, suddenly reminded that the big man hadn't put in an appearance on the beach that morning. Odd, he thought, for a guy who liked to keep the reins tight around his patch. 'Where is he today?'

'Day off, sir.'

'Right.'

Previously relaxed and chatty, the driver now tensely gripped the steering wheel and started staring rigidly through the windscreen, steeling himself to get a good word about his sergeant past his dry throat if the questioning continued.

But McCadden didn't pursue the subject. Having run his own checks over the last few days, he already had the rest of the answers that he needed. He knew that Mullaney's wife ran a thriving guest house in Dunmore. Small, razor-sharp and severely retentive, she was efficient with visitors, but sour and dismissive with her husband. It was the source of the big man's obvious frustration. But not a topic to gossip over with new recruits.

'What sports do you play?' McCadden wondered.

And luckily the driver was an enthusiast. It kept them occupied until they were approaching Waterford, when the driver gestured at the ambulance, which was still in front. 'Do you want me to follow it all the way to the morgue, sir?'

'Ah . . . no,' McCadden decided.

It was a little past noon. He'd arranged to meet the pathologist for a fuller report at three o'clock. And there wasn't much point standing around the morgue in the meantime, watching Craig dissect the corpse and ruining his own appetite. He was hungry. No breakfast. Worked through the morning on an empty stomach. All that healthy sea air . . .

'Drop me home, will you?' he said. 'I'll show you where it is.'

Around the corner from his flat, under the cannon openings of the Double Tower on Castle Street which had once defended the old walled city, there was a new Italian restaurant that he hadn't tried yet.

But McCadden, already behind on breakfasts, wasn't destined to have lunch either that particular day.

He made it to a table in the restaurant. He got past the

unsurprising menu, decided on minestrone and cannelloni, and was raising a glass of water to his lips when a waitress, a pad in one hand, a pen poised in the other, came and asked if he was ready to order. Before he looked up at her, as he laid the glass of water back on the table, he glanced out of the window.

And his attention shifted so dramatically, so comprehensively, that his fingers lost control of the glass and let it drop, spilling the water on the tablecloth.

On the opposite pathway, wearing a black baseball cap and a black Meat Loaf T-shirt, moving quickly and with his head down, Rookie Wallace was striding west, away from the centre of the city.

McCadden sprang up, making the waitress scream and drop her ballpoint. His chair toppled, caught the back of another chair behind him and crashed to the floor. A chubby head waiter materialized in his path on the way out, frantically waving his arms about.

'Is everything all right, sir?'

'It's fine, it's fine,' McCadden assured him. 'Garda matter.'

'Eh?'

'Police!'

Outside, for a moment or two, McCadden was oppressed by dark feelings. A disconcerting sense of *déjà vu*. A sensation close to the pointlessness of struggling in a nightmare. A fleeting fear that he was imagining things.

Because Wallace had disappeared again.

McCadden sprinted to the junction at the top of the short street. He stopped again at the second of the street's surviving fortifications, the French tower built by Huguenots in the late seventeenth century, and checked in all directions. Relieved, he saw that Wallace was on his right, just disappearing around the corner of one narrow lane and into another. Following at a slower pace, he reached the corner with the same distance between himself and Wallace and settled into a routine surveillance, confident now that Rookie was going to lead him to a little illumination.

But the tail turned immediately to farce.

Wallace swung right again at the end of John's Lane. He

completed a rough circle when he passed the entrance to Castle Street. He pushed on along Manor Street. And then stopped, after checking a note he carried in his left hand, right at the front door of the building where McCadden had his flat. Stooping, he examined the list of names against the row of bells, selected one, and pushed with his thumb.

McCadden sighed. Still walking at the same pace, he went on closing the gap between them, finally attracting Wallace's attention, and a furtive wave of recognition, when he was within a few metres of his own home.

'You knew I was following you, didn't you?' he said.

Wallace's ravaged, bullet-scarred face sneaked out a look of astonishment between the ridges. 'What's that supposed to mean?'

'Come on! You saw I was on your tail. Instead of leading me anywhere, you doubled back here. Give me a look at that note you're carrying that's supposed to have my address on it.'

Wallace glanced anxiously up and down the street, tugged the peak of the baseball cap a little deeper over his eyes. 'Could we, ah, go in, do you think? Before someone spots us.'

McCadden inserted the key in the lock and led the way upstairs and into his flat. Wallace followed him, but then stopped a little inside the door and stood there, checking it out. He studied the bedroom in the loft above his head. The open fireplace in front of him. The varnished floorboards. The shelves of books and LPs and CDs.

'Nice,' he said.

'You want a coffee, Tony?' McCadden asked.

'Love one.'

McCadden boiled enough water to brew a pot. Coffee was all he'd had that morning. More of it on an empty stomach wasn't exactly going to relax him, but there was nothing solid to eat in the flat. Shopping was among the ordinary routines that suffered during an investigation. Unless you had a dedicated partner.

He brought two mugs, milk and sugar back to the living room and found that Wallace was still standing in the same position.

'Sit down, Tony.'

Later, when he came back again with the pot of coffee and

poured into the mugs, Wallace was sitting in an armchair by the music collection, checking out the vinyl LPs. His mood seemed to have darkened. He had a copy of the Fairport Convention album *Liege & Lief* in his left hand and was reading the notes on the back sleeve with a sad, ironic smile on his lips.

'Do you remember the last track on this album?' he asked.

' "Crazy Man Michael",' McCadden supplied.

' "Crazy Man Michael",' Wallace repeated. He went on staring at the album cover, his eyes a little glazed, obviously not seeing either the print or the illustrations any more. He said, 'The first time I ever heard Sandy Denny singing "Crazy Man Michael" was a dull, windswept evening, late in July nineteen-seventy. I was eight years old. My old man had just bought this album, *Liege & Lief*. We were in the living room of our flat on St Christopher's Estate, down in Cork.'

McCadden drank his coffee. He poured another from the jug, stirred in a little milk and tasted it, while Wallace, as if marking the end of an overture, slipped the *Liege & Lief* album back to its place on the shelves, stretched out in the armchair, the heels of his sneakers resting on the front tiles of the fireplace and fell silent.

After a while, McCadden said quietly, 'This is going to take a lot more time than we actually have, Tony.'

Wallace nodded. 'Maybe.'

McCadden sighed. 'I mean, I was about to ask what you've been up to lately. If you're going to start at the age of eight and work upwards, the pressure on our time is bound to build.'

Wallace laughed a little. 'There's a point to it all.'

'I'm sure there is.'

'Do you mind?'

McCadden *did* mind. A middle-aged man searching desperately for his own father through the confused landscape of his inner feelings was one of those contemporary spectacles that invariably made him queasy. But he had problems to solve. And he couldn't choose the route to the answers. He asked dutifully, 'What was he like? Your father.'

Wallace shrugged. 'My old man? Slight young guy, with small, rounded features. Intense blue eyes. Afro-style auburn hair and a darker, heavy beard around his thin lips. A student's face. He'd finished a PhD in philosophy that summer. Heidegger, I think. Or Husserl. One of the existentialists.'

'I meant . . . as a person, I suppose.'

'I don't know. That's the only memory I have of him. Sitting in front of a turntable, between two massive speakers belting out "Crazy Man Michael", opposite a poster of Che Guevara stuck to the wall.'

'He died?'

'He left. Both of them. That July evening, almost thirty years ago now, the first time I heard Sandy Denny singing "Crazy Man Michael", that was also the last time I saw my parents. They left that night. Off to find themselves in Europe. Or gone to look for America. I never discovered which. And I haven't heard from them since. Maybe it was the spirit of the times. Freedom. Self-expression. Exploration. Or *one* of the spirits of the times. I remember standing at the window that day, the last time I saw them. Below me, on the square of green between the tower blocks that made up the corporation estate, a crude amplifier was pumping hymns through loudspeakers that had been strapped to five or six lamp-posts. I could hear both sets of music. "Crazy Man Michael" behind me. "Ave Maria" and 'Adeste Fidelis" and 'Faith of Our Fathers" in front of me. The old women from the neighbourhood, all of them dressed in black, were gathered around the lorry that carried the amp, clutching lighted candles in their hands and waiting for the arrival of the local priest, before setting off in procession around the estate. I could see my grandmother among them . . . That's how I know it must've been July the twenty-fifth, the last day I saw my parents. You know what July the twenty-fifth is?'

'No.'

'It's the feast day of St Christopher himself. Patron saint of travellers and hopeless cases.'

'Hasn't he been struck from the calendar?'

'Too true. But they never renamed St Christopher's Estate. I went back there for a visit a couple of years ago. It's swamped by heroin now. Every July the twenty-fifth the kids light a bonfire, throw a couple of stolen cars on to it and shoot up while sitting around it. Nobody remembers any more why they light a fire in the middle of summer, but that's all that's left of my grandmother's past, all that's left of her lighted candles and hymns and rosary beads.'

'And the point?' McCadden wondered.

'What?'

'You promised a point to all this.'

Wallace laughed. 'You haven't changed, have you?' he said. 'You still won't be suckered by emotions But yeah, there's a point to it all. The point is, I have very few beliefs left. I've no faith in individualism. That was the road my parents walked down. For the same reasons, I place no trust in the family, its values or its lifestyle. I can't commit myself to long-term relationships. And religion is dead. Even when I was eight, my grandmother's style of piety and devotion was no longer relevant. The only thing – beyond myself – that I've ever felt *comfortable* about is the state. For the first time in my life, I felt I *belonged* when I joined the force. You can understand that, can't you?'

McCadden grimaced a little, slightly embarrassed by this new sentiment. 'I know what you're saying.'

'You once told me that the notion of service was a sort of tradition in your family. I was impressed by that.'

'Yeah, well, maybe not as ... *comprehensive* a notion as the one you're advancing.'

'Nevertheless,' Wallace argued. 'Nevertheless ... ' He turned his face towards McCadden, his chin resting on his left shoulder, pushing the scar on his cheek up towards his sharp brown eyes. He said, 'Someone's been asking questions about me down here, haven't they?'

'Quite a lot of people at this stage, actually.'

'Inspector Tom Reynolds?'

'Among others.'

'What did he say?'

'Maybe you should tell me what you've been doing first.'

Wallace nodded, approving the strategy. 'The last six months', he said, 'I've been squatting in a vacant flat on St Anthony's Estate in Dublin. I blend in. It's quite easy. The trick is, not to pretend that you're one of them. You make mistakes with the slang and with the local knowledge and they spot you immediately. But I'm from Cork. I play the part of a gouger from Cork, tossed up on this estate after drifting for years. Who the hell knows whether I make mistakes with the Cork slang and who the hell cares whether I make mistakes with Dublin slang? That's expected of a Corkman. I keep my eyes and ears open. I don't get involved in crime, but I don't criticize anyone who is. Occasionally, the squat is used to stash dope or hide someone.'

'Reynolds is not chasing you around the country for that, is he?'

'No,' Wallace agreed. 'About a month ago – a couple of days before I rang you – I was sitting in the squat with two other guys from the estate, Willie Flanagan and Vinnie Woods. We were drinking cider and playing a little poker. Killing the time.'

McCadden felt a cold, clammy hand on the nape of his neck. He tried not to show his surprise. 'Who's Willie Flanagan?' he asked. 'And who's Vinnie Woods?'

Wallace shook his head. 'You don't know them.'

'I wouldn't ask if I did.'

'They're a couple of petty offenders. Flanagan is over the hill, but still does the occasional burglary. Woods is different. Seventeen years old and always flying on speed or crack or ecstasy. He's unstable. He's started running ecstasy and crack lately for a dealer on the estate.'

'So what happened?'

'Flanagan was dealing a hand of cards when we heard a racket from the flat above us. It was moving the light fitting on our ceiling, so that the bulb started swaying back and forth on the cord. Normally, you keep to yourself on the estate. But Woods insisted on going up to investigate that day. The flat above was also vacant. I think Woods knew it was being used for something, probably to stash some crack or heroin belonging to the gang he's associated with, and he was worried about it being discovered or stolen.

'I went upstairs with him. The door of the flat above us had been forced and it was hanging slightly open. There were no more sounds coming from inside. Everything was quiet now. We pushed the door a little wider and waited. When there was no response, we stepped inside. A few opened letters lay on the dirty floor, scattered around our feet. Beyond that it was just blackness.

'We had no torch. So we stopped and waited again. And we heard nothing. But as my eyes adjusted, I slowly worked out a blurred shape in the centre of the room in front of me. It seemed to be a chair, probably left behind by the people who'd lived there. It seemed to be damaged, listing to one side on a broken leg. And there seemed to be someone sitting on it, their arms dangling to the side, their legs sprawled in front. Woods saw him too and called out, *You got a problem, mister?* There was no answer. No movement.

'From behind, we heard the sound of Flanagan climbing the stairs after us, coming slowly and cautiously. But he'd brought a small torch.

'I remember the circle of light dancing on past to my left. It glided over the grimy floor, over the torn bills and envelopes, and picked out a limp human leg that was covered with white chinos, fawn socks and brown brogues. And it stuck there for a while. Because the chinos were so heavily soaked with blood that drops of it were falling from the hem and splashing on to the shoe and the floor underneath.

'Woods told Flanagan to lift the torch. But Flanagan was trembling by now. The circle of light travelled shakily upwards. Over the slack knees of the figure on the chair. Over the white golf shirt that had the manufacturer's logo to one side and a stripe of blood to the other. On to an unshaven, middle-aged face, with its skull crushed inwards around its right temple.

'The guy was still alive. But not by much. Just moaning softly.

'There were others still in the flat. Still in the darkness behind the chair. Watching Woods and Flanagan and myself.

'There was nothing we could do. We couldn't get involved. Even Woods realized that whatever he was protecting in the flat was now lost and had to be abandoned. We turned around and left the scene. In fact, we left the estate for the rest of the day, to get away from the heat.

'I waited for the story to break before deciding what I could do to help the investigation without exposing myself. But there was nothing in the news reports the following day. Two days later, after I'd bought an evening newspaper and was reading it on the way up the stairs back to the squat, I finally saw the injured guy's photograph. But the accompanying report said that he was missing after a boating accident and that the incident had happened in Dunmore East, more than a hundred miles from where we stumbled across him on St Anthony's Estate.

'I was so gobsmacked that I just pulled up with surprise. I stopped dead on the stairs.

'And the delay probably saved my life. As I stood there, I heard noises from the squat above. I crept up, just enough to peer over the stairway into the flat, and I saw six or seven of the local heavies waiting for me in the darkness inside, carrying baseball bats and iron bars.

'Someone had blown my cover. I learned later that they knew now that I was a guard, working undercover. It would have been a very neat murder.'

'Committed by who?' McCadden asked.

'Someone who already knew I was a cop. It's a small list.'

'Are you suggesting that *Special Branch* set you up?'

'Who else knew my real identity? You? Did you set me up? No, I'll settle for Tom Reynolds.'

'Why?'

'On a simple level, why else but because of the man in the chair?'

'You wouldn't remember his name, by the way, would you?' McCadden asked ironically.

Wallace laughed. 'Arthur Logan. Managing Director of Lisenter (Ireland) Ltd. Popular Irish-American businessman, well known in local circles in south-east Waterford County.'

'And on a complex level?'

'Why was Logan killed? I'm not too certain. I have my theories, but I'd like to hear your own ideas as well.'

'What about the others, Flanagan and Woods?'

'I got a message to them, warning them that I thought their lives were in danger. Whether they wanted to believe me or not, that was their own business afterwards.'

'Have you been in contact with either since?'

'No.'

'Would they know where you are?'

'If they saw the same news reports, I'm sure they'd make the same connections.'

'You rang me on July the twenty-eighth,' McCadden remembered.

'The same day I read the newspaper report. A couple of hours after I knew my cover was blown.'

'I was away on holidays.'

'So I heard.'

'I didn't get back until Monday last.'

'That explains that, then.'

'Why did you ask for information on Eleanor Shiels?'

'The reports linked her closely with Logan. She was the last to see him before the alleged accident.'

'Have you contacted her?'

'I couldn't risk it.'

'What did you learn?'

'A little about her background, about her career—'

'From a second-hand record dealer,' McCadden interrupted impatiently. 'I know. I don't mean her personally. What do you know about Logan's death?'

'Nothing,' Wallace said simply. 'I've been too cramped, too frightened to show my interest. Who can I trust? I don't actually *know* anything. I *suspect* that Reynolds is acting under instructions. It seems a reasonable deduction. I suspect that his master is Niall McAwley, the Minister for Justice. And because of the business and political connections between McAwley and Bill McMullan, the owner of Lisenter, I suspect that McMullan is the vulnerable one being shielded. Beyond that, I don't even have suspicions. I'm in the dark.'

'Why didn't you contact me again after the first call?'

'I discovered that you were away. I was waiting for you to return.'

'Look,' McCadden said wearily, 'you decided to lose me in town the day before yesterday. I know you saw me.'

Wallace shrugged. 'By then, Reynolds was closing in. I'm sorry, but as I said, I'm taking a risk trusting anyone. *Anyone.*'

'What made you change your mind? I presume our meeting today wasn't accidental.'

'I'm running out of time. The pack is closing in. I have no choice. I have to gamble. You're my best bet. Still a risk, but one with the odds tilting a little in my favour. I'm being honest with you.'

McCadden checked the time and the temperature of the coffee pot. He found that they both needed attention, but decided that they could probably be balanced if he moved quickly enough. 'Do you want another coffee?' he asked.

Wallace had drifted into a reverie of his own and started. 'What?'

'Coffee?'

'Yeah. Why not?'

McCadden collected the pot and the used mugs and carried them to the kitchen. He closed the door behind him. He needed space, a release from the pressure.

It all seemed so unlikely, he thought, as he put the water on to boil. So preposterous. And it all seemed to fit so neatly at the same time. It was simultaneously implausible and all too probable.

He poured a little boiling water into the coffee filter, absently watched the grounds expanding with the moisture and then carefully topped up the cone with the rest of the water.

And found that he couldn't get beyond the paradox he'd just described for himself.

A few minutes later, he lifted the pot of coffee from the machine and carried it back to the living room with a couple of fresh mugs. He poured, offered a mug to Wallace and stood while drinking his own.

Wallace watched him closely. 'You're sceptical,' he observed. 'Aren't you?'

McCadden tilted his head a little to one side and raised his eyebrows. *Anything other than scepticism would be insanity*, the gesture suggested. He said. 'It's too unlikely a scenario.'

'In what way?'

'It's too grand a conspiracy. Too inflated. We're a modest country.'

'Maybe your own mind can't grasp it,' Wallace suggested. 'Mine can easily get around the possibility that a popular American with an impressive civil rights record threatened to expose his boss and was murdered.'

'Murdered by whom?' McCadden asked a second time. 'By Bill McMullan?'

'By a politicized section of the police force, acting on the instructions of the Minister for Justice, a man who's convinced that his own destiny and the destiny of the people are synonymous and that whatever he does to serve himself will also serve the state. Think about it. Three people stumble innocently into this conspiracy—'

'And take refuge on my patch', McCadden interrupted ruefully, 'just as I'm applying to the Minister for Justice for promotion.'

'There are more important things than your career.'

'It was a joke,' McCadden said wearily. 'A joke.'

Wallace's intensity was starting to annoy him. His big theories. His sweeping embrace. His tales to rock the very foundations of the state. His tendency to see himself as the romantic hero, the minuscule thorn in the paw of the Celtic Tiger. His eagerness to become a symbol of rebellion and renewal and integrity.

The trouble with symbols, once you started believing in them, McCadden thought, was that it took a hell of a lot longer to expose and get rid of them than it did to uncover mere political corruption.

But perhaps his own irony, his preference for the smaller human scale, was also irritating Wallace.

He said, 'We don't really know one another well enough, do we?'

Wallace nodded slowly. 'I suppose I'm coming at this from a different angle,' he conceded. 'I've been sitting in a squat the last six months in one of the most squalid areas of the state, listening to the news and wondering who it is I'm supposed to be serving. Every day the reports are full of sleazy stories that wouldn't even have been imagined a decade ago. I'm sure you've heard them, too. Revelations that one of the little Napoleons who've run our affairs for so long isn't the charismatic statesman with the aura of command and the mythical presence that his lackeys have inflated him to, but only a cheap little spiv, bought by businessmen with greasy banknotes in clean brown envelopes to help them plunder the country's resources. Revelations that government Ministers have been enthusiastically immersed in graft and corruption and intimidation the last three decades. Revelations that state and charitable institutions, established to care for orphaned or illegitimate children, have routinely abused these innocents, often with political collusion.'

'I didn't say that your story was *surprising*,' McCadden pointed out.

'You wear surgical gloves whenever you touch any of the old icons in contemporary Ireland,' Wallace persisted. 'It's always rotten underneath and the slightest pressure breaks the brittle surface to reveal the squirming grubs.'

'I said it was *unlikely*.'

'In what way?'

'That's a pragmatic objection, not a moral one.'

'*Why* is it unlikely?'

'What, for instance, was Artie Logan doing in Dublin?'

'I don't know,' Wallace conceded.

'If they wanted to kill him and make it look like a boating accident, why take a detour through Dublin?'

'I don't know. My *guess* is that he forced their hand. My guess is that he'd arranged to meet someone in Dublin, perhaps an independent left-wing politician, who could help him. My guess is that a trawl through the independent politicians will turn up a contact.'

McCadden sighed and glanced at his watch. 'Talking about which,' he said, 'I've got to keep an appointment. Where are you staying?'

Wallace smiled sadly. 'I don't think I'd better tell you that. Not at the moment.'

'Right,' McCadden accepted. 'Do you want to stay here for the afternoon? It's safe and I'll be back around five o'clock. Do you want to do that?'

'Yeah, maybe ... Maybe I'll do that ... '

eighteen

Frank Ryan was already waiting at the morgue. As McCadden had anticipated, the examination of the scene at the Saleens after the removal of the body hadn't taken very long and had yielded nothing.

The only news that Ryan was carrying concerned the Special Branch detectives, Reynolds and O'Dea. Both had been in to view the body during the post-mortem, before Ryan's arrival. But neither had questioned the pathologist about the corpse before leaving again.

Dr Hugh Craig, still wearing a surgical mask, gloves and apron, and carrying a small plastic bag when he came out to meet McCadden, lowered the mask and dealt briskly with the query. 'They arrived in the early stages', he explained, 'as I was examining the back of the body. They waited until I turned it over. When they saw the face they left again. I imagined they were members of your own team.'

McCadden shook his head. 'No.'

'In any case,' Craig hurried on, 'I can now answer your earlier questions. The victim died between six o'clock on Tuesday evening and six o'clock on Wednesday morning. He was already dead when he entered the water. There are no signs of anoxia present. The cause of death was not drowning. He was actually killed by a stab wound to the left of his neck inflicted by a hunting knife or other broad-bladed instrument. Because there is only a single stab wound, with no incised wounds anywhere else on the body, and because of the near impossibility of so cleanly cutting a struggling person's throat, my opinion is that the stab was delivered while the victim was already unconscious. There are other injuries, but their cause is uncertain. The likelihood is that they occurred in the water. In any case, they made no significant contribution to his death.'

'Stabbed from the front or the rear?' McCadden wondered.

'From the front, and therefore by a predominantly right-handed assailant.'

'How much blood at the scene and on the killer?'

'Some. Not a great deal. The haemorrhage was almost entirely internal. The victim was a drug abuser, incidentally. Probably heroin. There are extensive needle marks on his arms and legs. I'll be able to give you more details, obviously, after the laboratory analysis.' Craig held up the plastic bag he'd been keeping. There was a small collection of stones inside. 'You said you wanted these,' he explained. 'They were taken from inside the remaining shoe on the victim.'

McCadden accepted the bag, slipped it open and looked inside, before handing it on to Ryan. He said, 'The body of a man named Arthur Logan was taken from the sea off Dunmore East last week. Did you also perform that post-mortem?'

Craig stiffened, expecting a complaint. 'Yes.'

'Could I ask you something about it?'

'Have you read my official report?'

'No.'

'I suggest you do.'

'I'm going to,' McCadden assured him. 'But the time lapse between getting an answer now or later could be important.'

Craig didn't so much loosen out – his rigidity just clicked from negative to positive. 'Very well. What is it?'

'Did Logan die from drowning?'

'Yes. Death was caused by asphyxia, due to sea water blocking the air passages. The indications are, however, that he may have been unconscious when he entered the water. There is little evidence of any intense struggle to save himself.'

'Was there an injury to the right side of his head?'

'Yes. A depressed fracture.'

'Caused by what?'

134

'The most likely explanation is one of the spars on the boat he was sailing, propelled by the wind or by some sudden movement of the vessel. It's impossible to confirm. Not all of the boat was recovered.'

'Could it have been a stone, a club?'

'Certainly not a stone. The wrong shape for the wound. A wooden club would be consistent, however.'

'Was it inflicted before he entered the water?'

'It seems so. Certainly before his death was caused by drowning.'

'This may sound bizarre,' McCadden cautioned, 'but is it possible that Logan was knocked unconscious some distance away, transported to Dunmore afterwards and *then* drowned?'

Craig tensed again, having suspected all along that the detective's interest was edging towards contesting his own findings. He said defensively, 'This was not a feature of the original investigation.'

'I know that,' McCadden accepted. 'And I know you're not bringing in the verdict. You only provided the medical evidence. But is it *possible*? Would it be consistent with your findings from the post-mortem?'

Craig squirmed. The movement travelled like a shiver through his tall, thin body, exhausting itself in a slight, nervous shake of the head. 'We have no reliable means of establishing exactly *when* the injury occurred, apart from saying that it preceded death,' he explained then. 'In that sense, therefore, your scenario is possible. Purely from a pathological perspective, I stress.'

'Well, as I said,' McCadden conceded, 'I haven't seen the file yet. It depends on when Logan was last seen alive, and who saw him. How long was he in the water?'

'Approximately two weeks.'

'You examined the body . . . when?'

'Last Thursday.'

'August the tenth. So, say he died . . . July the twenty-sixth, July the twenty-fifth?'

'Approximately.'

'Are you travelling back to Dublin today?'

'As soon as I'm finished with the present case.'

'Right. I may ring you later if I need to discuss anything further. That OK?'

'You have my mobile number, I believe.'

When Craig was gone, Ryan held up the plastic bag of stones and rattled its contents. 'I thought they were from a stony beach,' he said. 'Somewhere Woods was dragged along. But they're too regular, aren't they?'

'They're from a grave, Frank,' McCadden told him.

'Yeah?'

'Those little granite chippings that cover some graves?'

'Yeah, maybe . . . '

'I want you to go out to the cemetery at Corbally crossroads. Beside the spot where Cathy Morrison was attacked, you'll find another grave with the same sort of chippings. Take a sample and compare them. Rose Donnelly is already out there. Ask her to meet you and show you around. And bring a couple of uniforms with you to search the graveyard and the surrounding area. My guess is that *Woods* attacked Cathy Morrison. Apart from everything else – the time of his death, those little stones – she complained of feeling something cold against her face before she passed out. You notice the silver medallion Woods had dangling from his right ear?'

'What's a Dublin junkie doing down here, hanging around a rural graveyard?'

'I don't know.'

'Maybe I'll bring a dog as well, check the place for dope. He might have a stash he was visiting in the graveyard.'

'I think whoever killed him', McCadden said, 'also surprised him as he grabbed Cathy Morrison. It explains why she simply fell away from him and why there was no further assault on her.'

Ryan lifted the transparent bag and looked again at the stones, as if there was some magical guide to the truth in their arrangement. He said, 'But Woods died without a fight. So either he knew the character who'd just spoiled his fun, or he was overpowered himself. And if he was overpowered that efficiently, along with the neat way he was subsequently killed, it kind of points to someone with a fair degree of martial skills, doesn't it?'

'One other thing,' McCadden remembered. 'Who's back at the station right now that we can trust not to leak to Reynolds or the Chief Superintendent?'

'I'll check.'

'Right. I want them to get out the file on Artie Logan and contact me when they have it. I'll see you in Brownstown later. I've got to get something to eat. I haven't eaten all day.'

The same staff were still on duty in the Italian restaurant on Castle Street.

When McCadden strode in, the waitress examined him suspiciously, quickly confirmed her fears and then treated him like an advancing dog that *looked* domesticated but might bare its teeth viciously without warning. She slowly retreated, down the aisle, behind the front counter, and through a door that led to the kitchens. A second later, the *maître d'* peered out of the same door, his bald head dragging his bushy eyebrows upwards in surprise. And when *he* disappeared, the *waitress* returned, the exchange as synchronized, and as rigid, as the movements of plastic figures in a cheap weather clock.

The waitress seemed reluctant to serve. But perhaps a superior's hand started pushing her into the breach from behind. Because she eventually stumbled forward the first few steps.

McCadden tried to ignore the pantomime. He sat down, briefly checked the same menu he'd studied at lunchtime, but changed his mind about the meal and went for a more solid bolognese to comfortably fill his empty stomach.

He glanced at his watch as he waited. It was 5.47. He'd been awake almost twelve hours, he calculated. Probably the longest stretch he'd ever gone without solid food without being ill.

As he skipped mentally through the day's events, it occurred to him that he'd forgotten about his arrangement with Rookie Wallace. He was nearly an hour late already and stretching it further the longer he stayed in the restaurant. He groaned softly, cursing himself for not dropping back to the flat before eating. He could *ring* home, he thought. But Wallace probably wouldn't answer. And since the flat was only a minute's walk away . . .

McCadden stood up, just as the waitress finally reached his

table. From the look of dread in her pale blue eyes, it was obvious that this was like the recurrence of a nightmare to her. Even her scream was stifled this time.

McCadden looked at her apologetically. 'I'll be back . . . ' he started.

But it was useless trying to explain. The promise sounded like a threat. And even the helpless gesture with his hands made her recoil as he slipped past her.

Still wary that Reynolds might've put a tail on him that he hadn't yet spotted, he took the long way home, through the lanes Wallace had led him into earlier, watching his back and checking on the occupants of the parked cars along Manor Street. But he was clean, he decided again. Reynolds probably hadn't the resources yet for surveillance. Just himself and O'Dea, holding the pass until the cavalry flew in from Dublin.

But maybe not, he quickly revised. Maybe the pair *had* been here. Maybe they'd lit out because there was something more profitable to tail.

Because Rookie Wallace wasn't in McCadden's flat any more.

The records and the books he'd inspected earlier were all neatly back in their places on the shelves. Even the mug he'd used to drink coffee had been washed and dried and replaced in a cupboard. The other mug and the coffee jug were still sitting where McCadden had left them.

There was no note. No explanation.

It was as if Wallace had never visited.

He obviously hadn't panicked and fled, although the double life he'd led the last three years must've stretched his nerves by now. The exit was too contrived for that. So maybe he'd *always* intended splitting. Maybe he was testing reaction to the information he'd offered, watching and judging from a distance, ready to make contact again if he decided it was safe.

Whatever the explanation, McCadden could add nothing to it except useless speculation. He took a magazine to distract him and went back for a rerun of the pantomime in the restaurant.

And this time . . .

He'd managed to get the food on the table, the napkin on his lap, the fork and spoon in his hands, the waitress offering grated Parmesan nearby . . . when his mobile rang.

It was Liam de Burgh from the station, with the file on the death of Artie Logan. Not something he could defer.

'Logan was last seen locally on July the twenty-fifth, sir,' de Burgh reported. 'The last person to see him in the area was Eleanor Shiels. He visited her that night. He drove to Dublin for a business meeting the following morning. At least, that was the intention. He never arrived at his destination, although he rang from his own mobile phone that morning, July the twenty-sixth, to put off the appointment until the following day. He didn't keep the revised appointment, either. It was noted on the night of July the twenty-seventh to twenty-eighth that his car was abandoned, and unlocked, on the pier at Dunmore East and that his sailing boat wasn't in its berth. The car had not been there earlier, on the evening of July the twenty-seventh. The alarm was raised and he was presumed missing. When the body was recovered, there was a bruise—'

'Yes, I know,' McCadden interrupted. 'I talked to Craig. Was Logan drunk?'

'Very.'

'What about the last time Eleanor Shiels saw him?'

'Then, too.'

'Was there any blood in his car?'

'No, nothing suspicious about the car at all, apart from being unlocked.'

'Right. Thanks, Liam . . . '

'The Chief Superintendent is looking for you, by the way.'

'Right.'

The waitress had tired of holding the bowl of Parmesan and had left it on the table. McCadden's bolognese had cooled a little too much, but he sprinkled the grated cheese on it anyway and started eating. He couldn't really risk pushing his luck with the staff.

He didn't taste the meal. Didn't even taste the half-bottle of house red he had with it.

His mind was playing too intently with dates.

Wallace had phoned him on 28 July, the day Logan's disappearance was reported in the papers and the day *after* Logan's disappearance was discovered. That would make 26 July the date Wallace, according to his own account, stumbled on the injured Logan in a Dublin flat.

But what if Logan was in *County Waterford* on 26 July? Eleanor Shiels's neighbour. Sonny Newburn, said he'd seen Logan visiting the singer *a couple of days before his disappearance*. But was Newburn referring to the day the disappearance was *reported* or to the day the disappearance was *discovered*? And was he using *couple* precisely, to denote just two, or in the relaxed way most Irish people had with the term, to embrace anything between two and five? Did it mean he'd seen Logan on Brownstown Head on the evening of 24 July, 25 July, 26 July . . . ?

McCadden swore aloud in frustration. 'Shit!'

And it was typical of the sequence that the waitress returned to reclaim the Parmesan just as he cursed and that she took the obscenity as a judgement on the food.

nineteen

The theory was that Frank Ryan actually *enjoyed* detailed searches for evidence through difficult terrain. It was the only activity he could manage at the same pace as everyone else, the only time his bulk could comfortably meet the physical challenges of the job.

McCadden found him in the graveyard at Corbally crossroads, in the centre of a line of officers, plain-clothes and uniformed, who were painstakingly working their way through the graves and the headstones. It was their second time over the same ground. The first had been a broader sweep to establish if Vinnie Woods had been stabbed inside the cemetery itself. The consensus was that he hadn't. There were no bloodstains. In the absence of rain the last few days, spilled blood would've dried and stayed, both at the original scene of the knifing and along the route the killer must've carried the body.

What *was* confirmed, though, was that Woods had been in the graveyard and had probably been attacked there. His other shoe had been found in the high, untended grass on the rear perimeter, under the low wall that enclosed the graveyard. Almost certainly Woods's shoe, anyway. A mass-produced sneaker, it was true, but also the same make, the same style, the same size and from the left foot. Too much of a coincidence to believe that it was anyone else's.

It seemed that the sneaker had been picked up from where it had originally worked itself loose and then been tossed out of sight into the higher grass. Perhaps by the character who'd attacked Woods. Perhaps by some later visitor who found the litter offensive.

'You never know,' Ryan said to McCadden, holding up the sneaker in a plastic evidence bag. 'We might even lift a couple of prints from it.'

McCadden was more immediately interested in the fate of Woods. 'If he left the sneaker behind,' he speculated, 'it's likely he was carried or forced from here.'

'And killed somewhere else. But we don't know where. And we don't know how he was taken there. By car or on foot. Dumped in the sea. But we don't know where. And we don't know how. From a cliff or taken out in a boat.'

'We'll find out,' McCadden predicted. 'Tomorrow we launch a full-scale murder enquiry. You set up an incident room at the station in the morning.'

'Tomorrow's Saturday.'

'Nothing we can do about that. Call in anybody not on holidays. Rose Donnelly has already taken statements. Sift through them again.' He glanced at his watch. It was past nine o'clock. 'Maybe you should wrap up here in a while. Put someone on guard until you come back tomorrow. I'll see you at the station in the morning.'

McCadden drove away from the graveyard in troubled mood, able to make sense of Woods's presence in Waterford only if he accepted the accuracy of Wallace's account of what had happened in Dublin, only if he assumed that Woods had come to Waterford to look for Wallace. But it wasn't very convincing sense, he had to admit. If Woods had seen too much in Dublin, if he needed to go to ground to save his skin, why did he turn up in the one spot where the heat was most intense? What had he to gain by following Wallace to Waterford?

McCadden turned right off the main road and on to Brownstown Head. He went on past the staggered junction, with the entrance to the film set on his right and the winding road to the Saleens to his left, past Michael Constant's bungalow, and then slowed before easing on to the pot-holed track that led to the two isolated cottages at the tip of the headland.

There was no answer from Sonny Newburn's cottage when

McCadden knocked on its door, no signs of life inside. McCadden knocked again, but more from habit than determination. Turning away, he stepped from the pathway and walked across the grass towards Eleanor Shiels's cottage, reversing the route he'd taken in darkness with Sergeant Mullaney the previous Monday. This time her front door was closed against him, though, and there was no one at home.

Beyond the barbed-wire fence behind the cottage, a stocky farmer was leaning on a pitchfork in his field, surrounded by his adoring cows. Having enjoyably watched McCadden wasting time and energy, he now solemnly offered a blindingly obvious observation. 'They're not at home, you know.'

McCadden struggled with his temper. 'Right.'

'You'd be more likely to find them down at the filming.'

McCadden was surprised. 'Mr Newburn as well?'

'Except for Sonny. Sonny's away on holidays.'

'Right.'

'You'll find the woman, though.'

'The woman?'

The farmer jerked his head in the direction of Eleanor Shiels's cottage. 'Her!'

It was incredible, McCadden thought, how much venom the man could squeeze into such a small syllable. *Her!* He'd spat it out, an almost visible gob of green hatred.

It seemed to make him self-conscious, wary that he'd revealed too much. He suddenly softened, laughing loudly and saying, 'Ah, sure, you'll find them all down there tonight. There's a party on.'

The farmer's information seemed seriously skewed, though.

At first McCadden could find no one at all at the film set. Not even the two tenacious eco warriors. The barrier at the entrance was unguarded. And beyond it the car park, which had been teeming with cast and crew the previous night, now seemed deserted. The caravans were still there, but the people were gone. It was like a ghost town, an abandoned back lot.

McCadden walked around the barrier. Halfway across the car park, he heard faint voices coming from a caravan in a far corner and changed direction to head towards them. A figure in a dark suit, suddenly appearing at the top of the steps leading down to the beach, called him back.

'Carl!'

It was Paul Hyland, striding towards him with his usual Technicolor style, flashing teeth and diamonds at him.

'Did you get my message, Carl?' he asked.

McCadden shook his head. 'No.'

'I've been trying to contact you. The station can't raise you. And your mobile's not answering.'

'I'm off duty,' McCadden lied. He gestured around the empty car park. 'What's going on? Where's everybody gone?'

'They're packing up. Moving out tomorrow to some other location. The Wicklow Mountains, I think. That was always the plan.'

'I thought they were behind schedule?'

'They were, but three full days of uninterrupted sunshine cured that, as well as three full days of driving the crew like slaves. Are you heading down to the local pub? There's a going-away party there tonight. That's where everybody's at. You should drop down.'

'Right. What did you want to see me about?'

Hyland glanced around significantly. He touched McCadden's elbow to draw him away from the exposed centre of the car park towards the cover of an empty caravan. But it would've been foolish to read too much into the performance. Hyland's gestures were *always* too large and too colourful.

He said, 'Look, this is probably biting the hand, and all that. But shit, he'll be back in the States next week and I've got to go on earning and living down here. It was never my style to swing for somebody else's sins. The thing is, I'm going a little off Bill McMullan.'

'Now that the contract's up and the fee's paid?' McCadden suggested.

Hyland shrugged it off, completely unoffended. 'I don't like the way he pulls rank on the young women on the set. That's just a personal thing.'

'Any of them keeping your sheets too warm at night?'

'I *said* it was personal, Carl. But that's not it. The guy seriously

144

worries me. The night Cathy Morrison was sexually assaulted in the graveyard?'

Hyland paused. Possibly for effect. Possibly to ensure that they were still alone, still unobserved.

McCadden was impatient. 'What about it?'

'McMullan wasn't in his hotel room all that night,' Hyland confided. 'He said he was, but he wasn't. He slipped out and didn't return until after two. I just found that out today.'

'I thought it was Michael Constant who attacked Cathy Morrison, Paul?'

Hyland held his hands up to surrender the point. 'OK, OK. I swallowed that whole and served it back up to you. It was an idea kind of fed to me by McMullan himself. My fault.'

'Where's McMullan now?'

'Down in the pub, like everybody else. He's with Eleanor Shiels.'

'Eleanor Shiels?'

'Yeah. Something of a date, I believe . . . '

twenty

The pub was already overcrowded.

On a narrow platform to the left of the bar counter, a fat man was strumming an acoustic guitar, slowly picking out the first few bars of 'The House Of The Rising Sun'. No one was listening to him. They weren't attending to anything else either, though. They weren't even talking to each other. In fact, apart from the isolated guitar notes and the clink of glass from behind the counter, there was a tense, eerie silence in the place.

At first, after pulling the same stunt that had served him so well the last time he was here, by squeezing through the crush with the help of his ID, McCadden thought the resentment might be directed at himself. But his concern was wasted. A barman raised an eyebrow at him, mutely enquiring what his poison was, and then served him a vodka and white with a lack of interest that bordered on indifference.

McCadden drank. He looked around, trying to locate the source of all the uneasiness. But he couldn't. Apart from the bar staff, the elevated guitarist and the six or seven drinkers immediately hemming him in, no one else was visible from where he was standing. And none of his neighbours was familiar enough to chat to or sober enough to understand. The most likely, a tall farmer, still smelling of the cows he'd abandoned to join the session, stooped and squinted when asked what the problem was.

'What?'

'Why aren't the musicians playing? What's the problem?'

'No problem, boy. See the sign there? At the back of the stage?'

McCadden couldn't. The sign was too small. Or the guitarist was too wide. Or McCadden was too poorly positioned. And when he turned back to point this out, the farmer had been swallowed up by the crowd and replaced by a group of young crew members from the film set who were miming a miniature jive in the cramped conditions to some inaudible rock 'n' roll.

This surreal, soundless carnival boogied on for another five or six minutes, until the guitarist on stage finally slapped his palm across the strings of his instrument, severing the chord he was strumming and knocking harshly against the wood. It was a gesture of resignation and it was completed a few seconds later when the man slipped from the stool and left, without offering any explanation.

There was no response to his departure from the audience. No indication as to whether this was a welcome development or not. And the hand-painted sign at the rear, now clearly visible to McCadden, didn't offer any illumination either. TRA-DITIONAL SESSION, it read. EVERY FRIDAY NIGHT. LIVE MUSIC. None of its claims was particularly credible, but the last one struck McCadden as laughable.

The stage remained bare for a while afterwards. The crowd stayed tense and expectant.

And then the drama gradually unfolded.

From a distant corner of the pub, through a narrow channel that opened reluctantly in front of him, Bill McMullan led Eleanor Shiels on to the platform, his right hand gently holding the fingers of her left, his own left indicating the path ahead of them.

They looked like a couple, McCadden observed. Perhaps a professional couple. Perhaps a romantic one. But a *team*, in any case. Both were dressed in expensive suits. Hers was charcoal grey. His was black. In the centre of the stage, he lifted the stool the guitarist had used and placed it to the rear, clearing a space for her in front of the microphone. Then he silently presented her to the audience, bowed slightly, smiled even more faintly and left.

There was no approval. No cheers. No applause. But no one complained either. Or hissed. Or booed. There was just an awful, resentful silence.

And at last, McCadden understood the source of the night's tension.

Bill McMullan wanted Eleanor Shiels to sing. The locals didn't.

If Eleanor Shiels had been alone, she would've been prevented from performing. Given the mood of the locals, she might even have been physically attacked. Her political stance, supporting Michael Constant's campaign against the pharmaceutical plant, had isolated her from the community she'd come to live in. It had angered those who were previously indifferent. And it had reminded others that she was an outsider and would always *remain* an outsider.

The crowd's suppressed hatred was for her.

But Eleanor Shiels *wasn't* alone, of course. She was sponsored by the area's patron, protected by her own apparent enemy.

The crowd's *restraint* was Bill McMullan's due, therefore. Their respect was his entitlement.

It was a bizarre combination. And it quickly became even more involved.

When McMullan left her alone on stage, Eleanor Shiels adjusted the microphone, raising the bar from the low level the seated guitarist had used. She looked slowly around as she worked. From her elevated position, she noticed McCadden at the bar counter and nodded to him, smiling faintly. She finished her leisurely survey of the hostile audience. And then she closed her eyes and sang, unaccompanied.

As with her looks, her voice still held most of the power and the beauty that had captivated audiences in her late teens. It was older now, of course. It had to work a little harder for the more subtle notes. But it was also more mature.

She really was a magnificent sight, McCadden thought. This defiant woman in the centre of a hostile mob. Her head raised, her long black hair spread against the jacket of her grey suit, the sweat glistening on her upturned profile, the emotions of the song etched in the strain on her features. A woman full of life, full of personality, full of powerful passions. By comparison, what passed for beauty in the contemporary media was merely sad. All those bony, pallid supermodels. Those characterless fashion queens. And that frail prettiness of Cathy Morrison that was so attractive to the camera.

Even those posed photographs of Eleanor Shiels herself, McCadden thought. That sideways glance across the naked shoulder, against the movement of her body. They never did her justice. The plastic effect. The sheen. The artificiality. The contrived image clashed with her natural strengths. Was *that* the source of the tension that had destroyed her as a performer? he wondered.

But McCadden wasn't granted much time to indulge either his appreciation or his insights.

With the first line of Eleanor Shiels's song, someone in the audience behind him loudly cleared his throat and gave a low growl of disgust. He was one of the few to instantly recognise, not only the song itself, but also its complex theme. Because the number, echoing a tune that had been nagging consistently at McCadden all day, was Richard Thompson's modern ballad, 'Crazy Man Michael'.

Telling of a man who wanders alone in the forest, who meets with a raven and is driven wild by the bird's insistent prophecy that the man will kill his own lover . . .

The mood in the pub gradually shifted as Eleanor Shiels sang. It didn't soften. But the hostility was shot through now with grudging admiration. This was a moving performance, full of passion and conviction, and with a heavy sense of some hidden personal significance. The music carried the crowd with it, lifting them, if only for a short time, above the petty struggles of their ordinary lives.

One of the extras from the film had brought or acquired an acoustic guitar. After a tentative opening, he started supplying a soft accompaniment to the singing. Encouraged now by Eleanor Shiels's pause midway through the lyrics, he played the melody as an instrumental; until she came back in again for the final verses, still with her eyes closed, and sang of Michael's enraged strike at the raven's heart, his horrified discovery of his dead lover lying at his feet and his subsequent madness ...

The guitar didn't linger. It faded before the singer's voice had died away, as if it was humbly aware that anything else would be impertinence.

Eleanor Shiels stood afterwards in total silence. Even when she finally opened her eyes, it was impossible to tell whether she was satisfied or not. Impossible to gauge the effect on her audience. Impossible to read her intentions. Was she singing about self-destruction? About illusion and distortion? About the contemporary sorcery of film and pharmaceuticals?

Or was it, McCadden wondered – as Bill McMullan returned to the stage proudly to escort her off – was it merely a demonstration of how hopelessly McMullan was entangled in her artifice, how blinded he was by lust, how easy it would be to lure him, as the sorcerer had duped Crazy Man Michael, into suicidal error?

But entrapment was a dangerous gamble. It was double-edged. It exposed the deceiver to the same risks.

What if Eleanor Shiels was right about Bill McMullan? What if degrading submission in a woman *did* turn him on sexually? What if she could trap him only by making herself helpless? What then? What could she do to stop him brutalizing her? Unless there were others involved in the plan and waiting to intervene.

Just before Eleanor Shiels stepped from the rear of the stage, she turned and looked back, across the empty platform, over the heads of the crowds between her and the bar counter, straight into McCadden's eyes. And she winked at him. As if she could read his thoughts. As if she wanted him to *know* that she was reading his thoughts. And that she was dismissing his fears.

McCadden tried to return her signal. She didn't see the gesture. Or chose to ignore it.

As she stepped down from the platform and sank out of sight, he pushed away from the bar counter, intending to follow her. But the crowd was too dense. There was increased movement with the easing of the tension. Thirsty drinkers started to rush to the bar for refills. Another group of singers mounted the stage. They spent a few minutes in fluid confusion, but finally settled and started singing sea shanties. The session became more informal. The mood changed. The atmosphere suddenly relaxed. And even McCadden's ID no longer impressed.

He didn't see Bill McMullan or Eleanor Shiels again.

Frustrated, aware that the mood was lightening around him as his own humour darkened, he left the pub a little after ten-thirty.

It was still warm outside. Almost as warm as it had been inside the bar. People were standing around the forecourt and the rear car park, dressed in shorts, T-shirts, light dresses. Some he stopped to exchange a quick word with. Cathy Morrison. Bob Bettesworth. Sergeant Mullaney, stiff and starched in a dark navy suit, with his tiny wife weighing down his right arm and keeping his feet on the ground. None had seen Bill McMullan or Eleanor Shiels.

McCadden walked back alone to the graveyard at the cross-roads, where he'd parked the Mondeo earlier. The same route, it occurred to him, that Cathy Morrison must've taken the night she was attacked.

There was a uniformed guard on duty outside the cemetery gates, which were held together now with crime scene tape. Quite a few people had passed him during the last hour, the guard reported. But not Eleanor Shiels or Bill McMullan.

McCadden went to his car. On impulse, he swung it around after starting the engine, took an immediate right and drove down the rutted lane to Eleanor Shiels's cottage.

The place was in darkness.

He stepped out and walked again along the narrow pathway to the front door. There was no answer to his knock. And no answer from Sonny Newburn's cottage next door.

McCadden strode back to the idling Mondeo. He turned the car and travelled the short distance to the local hotel the film people were using. He asked a single question at the reception desk. And drew another blank. Bill McMullan wasn't there, either.

McCadden drove home.

He parked the car, climbed the internal staircase to his flat, checked that there was nothing of importance on the answering machine and stood on the bare floorboards in front of the fireplace.

He watched the clock.

Unable to eat, unable to rest, and not even interested in brewing a jug of coffee, he was kept awake, and agitated, by a nagging sense that something decisive was about to happen. It wasn't the usual feeling of anticipation that accompanied a detailed investigation. Not the hope of a break. Not optimism. More a fear of some sudden event. Something immediate and unexpected. Something dark and violent. Something he couldn't prevent . . .

Even when the hours dragged quietly by, even when the inactivity made the waiting tedious – way past midnight and into the early hours of the morning – he struggled to keep himself going.

He sat in the armchair in front of the fireplace. He took out the Fairport Convention album, *Liege & Lief*, and remembered Rookie Wallace. Wondered where *he* was, too. Wondered about the strange, blurred links between Wallace and Eleanor Shiels. The death of Artie Logan. The death of Vinnie Woods. The Richard Thompson ballad, 'Crazy Man Michael', which both Wallace and Shiels – coincidentally? – seemed to have adopted as their signature tune.

A whirl of connections that made no real sense . . .

twenty-one

The telephone was ringing.

An old-fashioned black Bakelite model he'd picked up cheap at some street market a few years earlier, it was sitting on the oak writing desk that was placed against the wall near the entrance to the kitchen. Its bell was loud and vigorous. But McCadden didn't *hear* it first. He felt its vibrations through the floorboards from where he was still slumped in front of the fireplace, and woke with the pleasant illusion that his feet were being gently massaged.

It was too fleeting a sensation, and quickly replaced by more painful ones. As he struggled out of the armchair to answer the call, he felt a sharp stab along the right side of his ribcage, from where he'd been lying awkwardly against the armrest of the chair. He was aware of a slight headache, too. And his brain was fuzzy.

Lifting the receiver, he searched for the clock to check the time. But he couldn't remember for the moment its location in the flat. He swapped hands on the telephone to glance at his wristwatch instead.

'Hello?' he mumbled.

His eyes were gummy. Rubbing them with the knuckles of his free hand to clear his sight, he peered again at the watch. It was three-fourteen in the morning, he saw. It meant little to him. He wasn't alert enough yet even to recall the sense of foreboding he'd carried into sleep with him less than two hours before.

'Carl?' the voice called from the other end of the line.

'Yeah?'

'It's Paul Hyland.'

And McCadden was suddenly awake, the surprise jolting him into consciousness, the urgency and anxiety in the other's tone alerting him. 'What can I do for you?'

'I'm not too sure. I just had this weird phone call from Bill McMullan.'

'Where is he?'

'He wants me to go collect him. I'm not sure I really want to get involved—'

'Where is he, Paul?'

'He's at Eleanor Shiels's place. Down on Brownstown Head.'

'What's weird about the call?'

'What?'

'McMullan wasn't driving. He was on foot. If he wants to get back to the hotel, he's looking for a lift. I know it's only a short distance and I know it's past three in the morning, but that must be part of what you're paid for, isn't it?'

'You don't understand, Carl.'

'Tell me.'

'I'm *trying* to fucking tell you! He doesn't just want me to pick him up. He wants me to get rid of evidence.'

'Evidence of what?'

'I don't know. He's drunk. Or drugged. He's rambling. He's snivelling down the fucking phone, for Christ's sake!'

'Saying what, precisely?'

'That he didn't mean it to go this far. That he never intended it. That it can all be tidied up. That's the sort of shit. And reminding me that I was a cop, that I know how to manage these things. This is what he's saying. I mean, fuck it, I'm paid to look after his security, but not that kind of shit. I want my back covered. That's why I'm ringing you. All right?'

McCadden felt a slight distaste. He searched for difficulties. 'There's no telephone in Eleanor Shiels's cottage.'

'He's on a mobile.'

'What's the number?'

'I'll give you the number, but he's closed it off. Dropped it or something. It's dead. I tried to reach it again after he rang off, but I couldn't.'

'When did he ring you?'

'Just now. Woke me up five minutes ago. I contacted you immediately. I'm being a good boy. Just remember that.'

'Right.' *Good?* McCadden thought. No. Cautious, maybe. Wily. Self-interested. 'Where are you now?'

'The film set. There's still a lot of gear down here that I'm responsible for. They're shifting it tomorrow. Do you want me to meet you at the cottage? It's only down the road.'

'No. Wait there. I'll contact you when I need you. He hasn't got any weapons, has he? McMullan. No guns or anything like that?'

'Not that I'm aware of. Maybe a knife, you know. That's about all.'

'Right.'

McCadden hung up and turned to leave. Already dressed, with his car keys and wallet still in his chinos' pockets, he stopped only to pick up a leather jacket, in case the night was cool outside.

But it was warmer on the street than in the flat. He threw the jacket on the back seat of the Mondeo, sat behind the steering wheel and turned the ignition, conscious of the noise he was making in the stillness of the deserted streets. The roar of the engine. The clanking of gears. The rush of tyres on the tarmac.

Someone else was restless that night. As he pulled away, a light went on in a top-floor window on the opposite side of the street and a sash was raised as the occupant looked out.

The traffic was too sparse to justify a siren, too thin to make running the red lights without one much of a risk. Within ten minutes McCadden was past the outskirts of the city, bumping along the lonely country roads that led to Brownstown Head. The journey seemed shorter than usual. Perhaps because he was so familiar with it by now. Perhaps because of the sense he had that he was hurtling towards some resolution, some dramatic shift in events.

Easing up at Corbally crossroads, he swung left, on to the headland. He knew that a uniformed guard was still stationed at the graveyard a little beyond, and that the guard had probably seen McMullan and Eleanor Shiels passing that night, but for once, McCadden decided to leave the questions until he knew what the hell he was asking about.

Around the corner he braked again. But gently. Softly. Not wanting to alert anyone to his movements. He switched off the engine and the headlights and let the car roll quietly forward in the darkness.

The headland felt eerie. The public lighting extended only a little past the entrance to it. Beyond that, it was total blackness. A sliver of moon seemed about to hide itself completely behind a cloud. And the invisible sea lapped quietly somewhere against the rocks and the shore.

There were no lights on in any of the houses.

McCadden waited until the Mondeo rolled to a stop just before the rutted lane that led to the last two cottages. He gently opened the door and left it ajar after stepping out. He took a torch from the glove compartment, but didn't switch it on.

By then, his eyes had adapted a little better to the darkness. Even from where he stood, a good thirty metres away, he could see that the front door of Eleanor Shiels's cottage was open. Still without a light to guide him, he picked his way through the potholes in the lane and turned in along the pathway to the cottage.

He didn't have to push the front door further open. The gap was already wide enough to slip through.

Once inside, he called out softly. There was no response.

Groping cautiously, he found the light switch on the wall to his left and clicked it on.

At first sight, the room looked much the same as the last time he'd been there. The Dali prints and African mask on the walls. The squat writing desk in the corner. The two armchairs in front of the fireplace. Nothing was damaged. Nothing disturbed.

The difference was minuscule. And almost perfectly camouflaged. On the upper panel of the varnished bedroom door, there was a short, narrow streak of what might've been red paint. Or lipstick. Or dried blood.

McCadden stopped. He took a pair of surgical gloves from his pocket and pulled them on. Switching on the torch, he quickly moved forward again. With the fingers of his right hand, he carefully pushed open the bedroom door. He took another step forward, over the threshold, and cautiously looked inside, probing with the beam of the torch.

In the centre of the crumpled white sheet that covered the bed there was a spreading pool of dark blood. From the middle of that pool, a thinner, more uneven streak was trailing to the edge of the cloth, over the side of the mattress, across the small white rug and on to the bare floorboards, where it finally faded. The brass bedstead bore four leather straps. Two at the head and two at the base. Presumably for tying the hands and feet of the captive who'd lain on it that night.

Beyond the bed Bill McMullan was slumped at the dressing table, where Eleanor Shiels had been sitting, dressed in a sleeveless blue slip, the first time McCadden had seen her. McMullan was unconscious. His right cheek was pressed against the surface of the table. His face was caked with powder from a ceramic jar he'd knocked over. His eyes were closed and his arms were dangling by the sides of the chair he was sitting on. He was breathing deeply, as if he was drunk, or drugged. On the floor between his splayed feet there was an empty plastic container that might recently have contained pills. Beside it there was a damaged mobile phone. And on the mirror above him there were handprints in blood, streaked at the base, where the hands themselves had slipped downwards or where the blood had coursed in rivulets along the smooth surface of the glass.

There was no sign of Eleanor Shiels. No sign of any of the clothes she'd worn that night.

McCadden reached out to his left again and switched on the overhead light.

Figure it out, he challenged himself.

The signs suggested that someone had been tied to the bed, injured in that position, dragged to the floor after being released, then wrapped to prevent further blood spills, and somehow spirited away. But McMullan had no transport. He had a car and a chauffeur at his disposal, of course. But if the hired help were willing to shift a dead or injured woman for him they wouldn't have abandoned him afterwards to his present condition.

So perhaps Eleanor Shiels had staggered out of the cottage under her own steam. Perhaps she was houseproud enough not to spurt any more blood around her better room. Perhaps she was lying out there on the headland somewhere, slowly dying by herself, too weak to drag herself further.

Or perhaps the blood was McMullan's . . .

McCadden couldn't see any obvious wounds on the American. But then, he had an odd sense that what he could see wasn't the best guide to the way things were, anyway.

So . . . perhaps the blood *was* McMullan's. Perhaps the pills had been *administered* to him, rather than taken by him.

Perhaps . . .

It took only five minutes for the first of the mobile patrols to reach McCadden after he'd called for back-up. Within thirty, he had a score of uniforms under his command, a scene of crime team a couple of kilometres away, a police doctor examining McMullan, and some early answers to a few of his questions.

Eleanor Shiels wasn't lying in darkness in the immediate vicinity of her home. Or anywhere else on Brownstown Head. She'd disappeared. And Bill McMullan couldn't throw any light on her whereabouts. Or not tonight, anyway. He'd taken an overdose of his own sleeping pills.

'When can I talk to him?' McCadden asked the doctor, as paramedics were frantically wheeling the American on a stretcher towards the waiting ambulance.

The doctor looked aghast. 'Talk to him?'

'It's important.'

'You don't understand, Inspector,' the doctor snapped. 'This man could die.'

'I need to be kept informed.'

'If he dies?'

'As soon as there's any significant change in his condition.'

twenty-two

But Bill McMullan didn't inconvenience anyone by passing on that night. In fact, McMullan didn't even stay asleep for very long.

A little before six o'clock, after interviewing the guard on duty at the graveyard and wandering back to Eleanor Shiels's cottage to check on the progress there, McCadden was in the middle of an awkward exchange with Sergeant Mullaney when he took a call from the duty doctor at Waterford Regional Hospital.

Mullaney was supposed to be helping at the crime scene. McCadden found him by the squat writing desk in the front room of the cottage, shuffling avidly through the erotic photographs of Eleanor Shiels.

The sergeant's interest seemed more private than official. His lips were dry and his breathing was slow and heavy. And he was so absorbed that, once again, he was unaware that his lust was a spectacle.

McCadden coughed.

The big man started. The photos spilled from his gloved hands and fell, scattering around the floor by his feet, and causing him even more embarrassment as he bent his enormous frame into an ungainly crouch and tried to gather the slim prints with clumsy gropes. When he stood up again, he was actually blushing. His hands were shaking. He looked more dangerous than cowed, though. More furious than contrite.

Flapping the thin stack of photographs in the air, he said desperately, 'Artie Logan, sir.'

It was probably only an unconscious effort to offload guilt, but it startled McCadden. He instantly abandoned any interest in ethics. Significant information seemed to be on offer. 'What about him?' he asked.

'These photographs, sir,' Mullaney explained. The sergeant could obviously *feel* that he was wriggling off the hook, but he didn't understand *why* yet and had to be careful not to snag himself again. 'They were taken by Artie Logan.'

'Are you sure?'

Mullaney nodded vigorously. 'The negatives were at his house when we searched there after his disappearance. I itemized them myself.'

'Look,' McCadden warned, 'I'm not interested in anything else here. Do you understand? So let's be clear. Are we talking about this precise set of prints?'

'Yes, sir. They were there. He developed them himself. There were a lot of others, too. Well, not of women or anything like that. He was involved in photography. I think he had a local study group. Or he ran local classes, or something . . . '

McCadden's mobile phone rang. It was the control room at the station in Waterford, telling him the duty doctor at the hospital needed to contact him urgently and was holding on another line.

'Can you put him through?' he asked.

'It's a woman, sir.'

'Well, put *her* through then.'

Her news was surprising.

Bill McMullan, courtesy of a freshly pumped stomach, was unexpectedly awake. Not quite ready to leap back into the saddle just yet, but certainly out of danger. The trouble was – at least from McCadden's point of view – that McMullan was also insisting on leaving. In fact, he was already dressing himself as the doctor was talking. And while the medical staff could recommend rest and recuperation, they could hardly forcibly detain a reluctant patient . . .

McCadden thanked her. Quickly raising the two uniformed guards he'd sent in as escorts for McMullan, he chewed their ears off when he discovered that they were sitting contentedly in the corridor outside the ward sharing jokes and morning coffee, and he left them with the assurance that their necks were on the line if they allowed the American to slip away.

'Put those photographs in an evidence bag for me,' he ordered the still apprehensive Mullaney after ending the call. 'And get the negatives. Where are they?'

'Still at Mr Logan's house, sir. He lived alone. His executor hasn't quite decided—'

'Right. You can seize them as evidence, if necessary. And clear a path for me to get my car out of here, will you?'

This time McCadden used the siren on the return journey to Waterford. Frustrated at first by the number of tractors and other farm machinery on the country roads, he made smoother progress once he hit the outskirts of the city again.

At the hospital the two uniformed officers were now standing stiffly to attention in the warm corridor. Only their facial muscles, loosened into expressions of relief, were even *slightly* relaxed. For the moment, they were off the hook. Bill McMullan, after an early attempt to shake them off had failed, was occupying his private room again.

McCadden moved on after catching their report, looking for the doctor he'd talked to. She was a young black woman, originally from Lesotho, afflicted with a couple of dense personal and family names which he didn't have the time to learn how to pronounce properly.

'Mr McMullan', she explained to him, 'took a dose of tranquillizers sufficient to induce sleep, but not in any quantity large enough to be dangerous. The drugs were prescribed by his own doctor. Since he's familiar with their effects, it's doubtful if this was in any way a suicide attempt.'

McCadden shrugged. 'Maybe he didn't have enough.'

She held up a small plastic container between the thumb and forefinger of her right hand. The cylinder was crammed with pills. 'This was in his pocket.'

'Right. Can I talk to him?'

'We've advised him to remain in the hospital for observation.'

'I understand that. But can I question him without the risk of inflicting brain damage?'

'I don't foresee any such difficulties, Inspector.'

'Good.'

When McCadden knocked and went in, McMullan was pacing up and down the bedroom. The American was already dressed. In the same black suit he'd worn the previous night, McCadden noticed. With no bloodstains on it.

McMullan didn't stop pacing. He glanced across at McCadden and nodded slightly in greeting, both without breaking stride, then turned at the window and walked quickly back towards the bed.

McCadden sat on one of the chairs that had been placed by the bedside for visitors. He said, 'Do you remember what you did last night after leaving the pub?'

McMullan stopped by the window and looked out, his back to McCadden. Without turning, he asked bluntly, 'Why?'

'You were seen by the officer on duty at the graveyard passing there a little before midnight. Do you remember what you did then?'

'Why?' McMullan demanded again.

McCadden didn't continue this time, forcing the other to turn. The American looked mostly irritated and impatient, and otherwise puzzled. There was no fear. But he couldn't seem to prevent himself from glancing frequently at his Rolex watch.

'Do you know how you ended up in here?' McCadden asked.

'No.'

'Right,' McCadden accepted. 'Neither do we.'

McMullan frowned. Presumably because of the face-lifts he'd endured over the years, the ripples were shallow on his suntanned forehead, the effect like a slight creasing in plain brown paper. 'You don't?' Knocked off balance for a second, he then saw through the ruse and quickly recovered. 'Yeah, well,' he said, 'I reckon you'll work it out.'

'Aren't you curious?'

'About what?'

'How you got here.'

'No. So unless you got something crushing your chest you need to heave off, I guess you'd better excuse me. I got to get out of here.'

'And Eleanor Shiels?'

'What about her?'

'You spent the evening with her. You were seen in her company by the officer at the graveyard, after which you went with her to her cottage on Brownstown Head.'

'She tell you all that?'

'Eleanor Shiels has disappeared, Mr McMullan.'

For a second, McMullan's reaction was revealing. He wasn't surprised. But then his brain kicked in with a warning and supplied the recommended response from a concerned acquaintance. He frowned again. 'How do you know?'

'We think she may have been abducted. Perhaps even killed.'

'I reckon not, Inspector.'

'No? There are signs of a struggle at her cottage, bloodstains on her bed sheets.'

'Bloodstains?'

'You were probably the last person to see her last night.'

McMullan put his hands in his trouser pockets, feigning an ease that he couldn't be feeling. 'Let me get this one straight, Inspector,' he said. 'Am I under arrest here?'

'I'm asking for your assistance.'

'OK. So I'm free to get you off my back and hike my butt out of here? As of now?'

'If you do, you may be taken in for questioning.'

'Yeah?'

'The alternative is to answer my questions here.'

McMullan started nodding his head in a series of rapid, nervous movements, a gesture of acceptance that Americans seemed to use to express extreme agitation bordering on explosive confrontation. He looked at that Rolex watch again and said, 'I've already contacted my attorney, Inspector. If you're not placing me under arrest right now, would you get the fuck out of my room and wait for him in the lobby?'

McCadden stood up. 'Sure,' he said cheerfully. One of the half-dozen monosyllabic Americanisms he'd picked up from watching reruns of *Friends* and *Frasier*, it seemed the most appropriate in the circumstances.

Lawyers never bothered McCadden. Not by themselves, anyway. But this one, an unfamiliar little grey-suited terrier from out of town somewhere, had stacked his team and brought a whole *army* with him to the hospital. A *procession* of obstacles, advancing in single file down the narrow corridor.

Among them was Chief Superintendent Cody, clearly on official business, but not in his uniform. A disturbing departure for a man so addicted to the regalia of rank. And behind the Chief Superintendent waddled Bill Toppin, a fat elephant of a local politician, who boasted the unhelpful combination of bearing a grudge against McCadden and being a close associate of the Minister for Justice, otherwise chairman of the internal appointments board, and enthusiastic McMullan fan, Niall McAwley.

The assault unit seemed to have rehearsed their separate functions. There was an almost military precision about the way they fragmented on arrival. The lawyer went straight in to McMullan. Toppin took up sentry duty outside, his massive bulk comfortably blocking the entire doorway. And Cody drew McCadden away from the action, to an isolated section of the corridor.

The Chief Superintendent's complaints were predictable. He expected to be notified by his own officers, he fumed, not by outsiders. Hadn't he requested McCadden to contact him for instructions the day before? And apart from everything else, the Special Branch officers from Dublin were still awaiting McCadden's report, having gone past hoping for normal co-operation . . .

'It's Saturday,' McCadden pointed out. 'It's still early in the morning. I don't know myself what's going on.'

'That's not a decisive criterion. Not in a case of this magnitude, this sensitivity—'

'Right.'

'Have you arrested Mr McMullan?'

'No.'

'Please wait here until I return.'

Cody strode away, knocking on the door of McMullan's room

and awaiting an invitation to enter, like a nervous bell boy in a cheap hotel. Too long in the tooth to feel resentment, McCadden was still irritated. Cody made the same annoying call time after time. Enthusiastic about raids on local authority housing estates, he withdrew the antennae as soon as they touched the privileged and the powerful. Maybe it was the price you paid for higher office. Knowing who your masters were.

With his usual eye for an opening, Bill Toppin waddled down the corridor to gloat, an outsize caricature of a parliamentary heavy.

McCadden didn't wait for the fat man to put the boot in. He asked cheerfully, 'How's zero tolerance coming along, Mr Toppin?'

This was the crime-fighting policy that Toppin's party had feverishly promised the electorate during the last campaign, and then fucked out the window as soon as it had attracted them enough nervous votes to form a government.

Toppin gave a pained smile. It wasn't any reliable indicator of his thoughts or feelings. Because of his excess weight, *all* of Toppin's movements were pained. 'How's your career, Inspector?' he countered.

McCadden shrugged. 'I have to admit, not rising as spectacularly as the rate of white-collar fraud. Although there should be a proportionate relationship.'

'You think you're funny, don't you?'

'No. There are very few things I think are genuinely funny. I'm not one of them.'

Toppin looked furtively around, preparing to share an insider's confidence. 'Let me tell you, Inspector, on the QT, straight from . . . well, the Minister himself.'

'I thought you were going to say *the horse's mouth*.'

'Your chances of being appointed head of the new Murder Squad are nil.'

'That's why I'm on the shortlist, I suppose.'

'That's only for the pleasure of watching you raise your hopes and having them dashed.'

'A pleasure you've now spoiled', McCadden pointed out, 'by letting me in on the secret.'

The Chief Superintendent returned before the exchanges could get any dirtier. He stood silently for a while between Toppin and McCadden, clearly waiting for the politician to drift courteously away. But Toppin didn't budge.

'I have Mr McMullan's assurance', Cody said then, 'that he will present himself at the station at four this afternoon to answer any outstanding questions you may have.'

McCadden raised his eyebrows. He said bluntly, 'I need to interview him now.'

'That's not acceptable.'

'*Acceptable*? To who?'

Cody joined his hands in front of his body. It was a gesture of closure, of exclusion. 'Thank you, Inspector,' he said coldly. 'I expect to see you in my office at three-thirty.'

'Three-thirty,' McCadden repeated. He knew that Toppin must be smirking by now, but he didn't want to give the fat man the added satisfaction of displaying his smugness. He walked away without looking again at either Toppin or Cody. 'Right . . . '

It occurred to him, given the mood of his departure, that he was probably walking away from the chance of promotion as well. But as Rookie Wallace had said, there were more important things than one's career. And McCadden was beginning to give more thought, more scrupulous attention now, to the words of Rookie Wallace . . .

twenty-three

McCadden drove west across the city after leaving the hospital. Skirting the trading centre, which was starting to come alive for the Saturday morning shoppers, he started climbing Patrick Street as the bells were pealing in one of the nearby churches. On Ballybricken Hill, instead of turning into the station car park and reporting in, he drove straight on, down the Glen, into Bridge Street, and across the bridge spanning the broad River Suir. On the opposite side he swung left, taking the main route to Dublin, 170 kilometres away to the north.

He called the control room once to patch him through to Frank Ryan and asked Ryan to cover him for the rest of the day. Maybe for the whole weekend, he added. It depended on how things fell out.

'Bill McMullan is coming in at four this afternoon to make a statement with his solicitor,' he explained. 'I've got a list of questions. He won't answer them, but we need to ask anyway.'

Ryan jotted down the queries and wondered, 'What's officially wrong with you, by the way?'

'Exhaustion. Working all night. Home in bed.'

'OK.'

'Any news?'

'No developments with Vinnie Woods. No news on the whereabouts of Eleanor Shiels. No definite line on the source of the blood in the cottage or the weapon that caused it. The only thing, and it's probably not adding to what you know, is that the handprints on the dressing-table mirror are definitely

McMullan's. They were on the dressing table itself where he was lying as well.'

'There's no blood on his clothes, Frank.'

'Well, apart from the dressing table and the bed, there isn't any on the other surfaces in the cottage bedroom, either.'

'Funny, isn't it?'

'Hilarious,' Ryan agreed. 'Are we arresting McMullan?'

'Not a hope, I reckon. Just ask the questions and note his answers. Leave the decisions to Cody. You won't be able to reach me, so I'll get back to you later today.'

McCadden switched off the radio afterwards, slipped a tape in the cassette deck, and listened to a Garbage album as he drove.

Perhaps it was the maverick nature of the move he'd made, severing any contact with base, but the further he got from Waterford the lighter he felt.

He'd served there for too many years now, he reckoned. Burdened himself with too many intimate memories. And managed to get himself so settled, so accepted, that he was no longer a stranger in the city. He needed to move.

Looking back after crossing the river, he'd framed for an instant in his rear-view mirror the standard view that turned up on all the picture postcards and all the promotional literature for tourists. The city's wide stretch of quays, the merchant ships on the water and Reginald's tenth-century tower in the background. There was a valedictory feel to the glance. But whether its source lay in optimism or fatalism . . . it was hard to tell.

He stopped in Carlow for breakfast, neatly splitting the journey into two fairly equal parts, and drove on afterwards in more relaxed shape, through neutral country. It wasn't until he hit the carriageway on the main approach to Dublin, entering territory where he'd once fought other battles, that he had the sense again of re-entering his own life and was reminded of the purpose of his journey.

The traffic was heavy on all three lanes coming into the capital. He'd already planned a route to Kevin Street Garda Station, and was thinking about adjusting it slightly, when he pulled up at a red light, glanced across at a passenger in the adjacent Saab who was reading a daily paper, and was reminded that it was Saturday. Chris Smith, the detective he needed to contact, wouldn't be on duty that morning. Wouldn't be back at his desk until Monday.

Time was always a personal experience, of course. But pursuing a private obsession, McCadden reflected, sometimes made you lose sight even of the standard calendar.

It was almost eleven by then. Smith lived on one of the new middle-class housing estates in the prosperous south of the city, and by mid-morning on Saturday would either be shopping or gardening, sleeping or watching TV. Not difficult to track down, anyway.

The estate turned out to be a cul-de-sac. It suited McCadden. Remembering the mysteries that had balked his last attempt to reach Smith and the paranoia of Reynolds and O'Dea in Waterford, he worried that Special Branch might have surveillance on his friend.

He took a leisurely cruise around the circular green in the centre of the estate. Reckoning that all the nearby houses had front gardens that were too well tended to show the uncaring hands of undercover cops, he spotted only one parked car with a driver inside. And even that was quickly explained. It was only a teenager, nervously waiting for his even younger girlfriend to be released by her parents.

When McCadden pulled up on his second spin round, got out and rang the bell of Smith's house, a redheaded boy of eleven or twelve opened the door. Behind him, drying her hands on a tea towel and trailing a girl of about nine, the boy's mother came down the hallway from the kitchen.

The kids were curious. *Only* curious. And quite open about their nosiness. And Sandra Smith, who knew McCadden from the time he'd served in Dublin, looked only surprised at first and then pleased.

So no one was uptight. No one had been warned or alerted.

Family life, McCadden thought wistfully.

Chris Smith was one of those cops, among the vast majority on the force, who diligently put in his eight hours and his five days, and left it all behind him when he went home. Had his family, his football, his golf.

It was a balance that McCadden could never manage to achieve. He wasn't driven by the urge to further his own career and clamber up the promotion ladder. In a job where you needed to look out for one another, that kind of thick-skinned ambition only made you an unreliable arsehole. It was a temperament thing. Worrying over a problem, he found it tough to let it go.

Smith, a redheaded countryman, spreading around the waist a little from too much desk work and not enough time in the field, was watching horse racing on the TV in the front room. When his wife and two kids escorted McCadden in, crowding the doorway behind him, he turned away from the set with the glee of the small-time punter who'd just taken another fiver out of the bookies, and only gradually rearranged his face to accommodate astonishment. Half-rising from the chair, he muttered, 'Jesus, Carl . . .'

The door was closed discreetly behind McCadden, leaving him alone with Smith. He shook hands and said, 'I've been trying to contact you. I left messages for you at the station.'

Smith frowned. 'When was the last one?'

'Couple of days ago.'

'I didn't get them.'

'Someone's playing funny games, then. I also left a message on your answering machine here.'

'I got that, but I thought . . .'

'Remember yesterday week, when I asked you to run a check on a character named Rookie Wallace?'

Smith sat down, muted the sound on the TV, and gestured McCadden into another armchair. 'Yeah, I remember.'

'You never got back to me.'

Smith spread his arms, gesturing his surprise, his helplessness. 'Nobody told you? he asked.

'Told me what?'

'Shit! Listen, I . . . I mean, I ran the check on Wallace. No record. I asked around. I don't know him myself. One of the lads familiar with that area, I asked him. Next thing I know, the super's calling me into his office. There's a couple of Special Branch fellas in there with him. What's my interest in Rookie Wallace? Leave it drop. It's an internal security matter. Very sensitive. Inspector McCadden in Waterford will be notified. Don't contact him until you're instructed again.'

'Right,' McCadden said. 'That's what I thought.'

'Did I land you in something?'

'No, no. Nothing to worry about. Do you know a guy called Willie Flanagan, Chris?'

'Willie Flanagan? Small, weaselly fella? About forty?'

'I don't know. I never met him. He might hang out with another guy called Vinnie Woods.'

'Yeah, that's him. I know Flanagan, all right. Small-time gouger. In and out of prison. Six-month, nine-month stretches. That class of thing. Shoplifting, mostly.'

'And Vinnie Woods?'

'Different proposition altogether. Seventeen, eighteen years old. Lives in the same place as Flanagan. St Anthony's Estate. But he's a fucking junkie. So into anything'll make him enough to feed the habit.'

'Woods's body was taken off a beach in County Waterford yesterday morning, Chris. He was knifed and thrown into the sea. You obviously hadn't heard.'

'Good riddance,' Smith greeted the news. 'That what you're here for?'

McCadden shook his head. 'I'm not officially here at all, Chris.' He hesitated, looking around the room, at the neat walls that were crowded with photographs of the family. Holiday snaps. School groups. Studio portraits. And at the angle he was seeing things just then, all the faces seemed to share the same disapproving expression. He said, 'I just want you to tell me where I can find Flanagan.'

'No, I'll take you there,' Smith offered.

'It mightn't work to your advantage.'

'You don't have to tell me what's going on, but it's not a place you'd walk into without covering your back. I can't let you do that. OK?'

'Appreciate it.'

'Have you got a gun?'

'No.'

'Not to worry.'

twenty-four

McCadden remembered St Anthony's Estate as a black spot.

A complex of local authority flats laid out in chunky tower blocks, it was fenced around with steel and accessible by car only through a single approach road. Its enclosed design isolated its community. It also turned the place into a fortress, easy to defend and difficult to raid or patrol. Predictably appealing to the street criminal. Even the best of its people, disillusioned by the conviction that no one could even see them any more, had to motivate themselves and their kids to keep up the daily contact with the outside world, where all the jobs and the schools and the services lay, not quite out of reach, but far enough away to question the effort.

The news was, the place had gone downhill in the six years since McCadden had seen it. Its best had given up on it and drifted out to improve themselves elsewhere. Strong-armed local opposition to drugs had flushed the dealers and the junkies out of other estates nearby. With its weakened community, its isolation and its surfeit of vacant squats, St Anthony's had become one of the main centres for trading in heroin and crack.

Smith and McCadden parked on Erris Road, close to the shopping district, and walked from there on to the estate. To match McCadden's already casual outfit, Smith had squeezed into his oldest jeans and T-shirt. He needn't have bothered. They were instantly recognized as cops. A few of the tough-looking kids who were hanging around the entrance to the estate sauntered challengingly across their path, trying to provoke a response. The rest scurried off to warn the druggies that there were pigs in the area.

From a distance the towers didn't look so bad. The exteriors had been cleaned and painted recently by the local authority. But the image was deceptive. All the dirt had been swept inside the buildings.

The doorway of the tower where Willie Flanagan lived was half blocked with rotting garbage and soiled plastic nappies, its stench rising powerfully with the intense heat of early afternoon. The lift inside wasn't working. And the stairway to the fourth floor was covered with litter and obscene graffiti, some of it scrawled with excrement.

Every time the detectives turned a corner on their way up, another scrawny, shadowy figure slipped out of sight ahead of them and anxiously watched their progress from the darkness. Smith didn't comment, but the disgust was written on his face. Knocking loudly on Willie Flanagan's grubby door, he held his ID up to the spyhole for inspection and then spat on the ground while waiting to be admitted.

The guy who opened the door looked closer to sixty than to forty. He was small and shrivelled, with a creased, unhealthy face. He had the crouch of a supplicant, which he never seemed to straighten from. His brown hair was thin, his eyes were watery and his skin was dry.

'How are you doing, Willie?' Smith asked rhetorically. 'Detective Sergeant Price sent me along. You know Sergeant Price, don't you? Are you alone, Willie?'

'Wha'?'

'Anyone here with you?'

'Naw. Just meself, like.'

'Good man.'

Smith had explained that everything inside the flat was either nicked or bought with stolen money. The effect on the decor was weird. The bulkier items, like the table and chairs, were all cheap and grimy. The portable stuff was better quality. The stolen Sanyo TV, for instance, tuned to a Saturday afternoon sports programme, was perched on top of an upturned wooden fruit box. And the stolen weather clock on the wall inside the front door, accurately saying it was thirty-two degrees, was positioned directly over a jagged hole in the concrete floor.

'This is a friend of mine, Willie,' Smith explained. 'Detective Inspector McCadden. He has a few questions for you.'

Flanagan sat at the rickety, Formica-topped table and started rolling thin cigarettes from the papers and tobacco already lying there. It was a nervous habit. Within minutes, he was rolling them faster than he could burn them and laying out the surplus in equilateral triangles on the table.

'Questions?' he repeated. 'About what?'

'How's Vinnie Woods, Willie?' McCadden wondered.

'Vinnie? I don't know. OK, I suppose.'

'When was the last time you saw him?'

'The last time?' He had an annoying habit of echoing a few words from the previous question to buy a little time. Useless time, really. Because he wasn't much of a thinker. 'A few days ago,' he said. 'Yeah, I had a jar with him a few nights ago. Maybe last week. Last Saturday, that was it.'

'Where is he now?'

'Now? I wouldn't know that.'

'But you know Rookie Wallace?'

Flanagan shifted uneasily. He sucked the burning tobacco a little closer to his brown fingers and said, 'Rookie? Yeah, I know him. He kips in one of the other blocks.'

'Are you and Vinnie and Rookie ever together?'

'Together?' With his bony thumb and forefinger, Flanagan pinched a fleck of stray tobacco from his dry lips and asked nervously, 'What are you tryin' to pin?'

'I don't know. What is there to pin?'

'Nothin'.'

'How about back towards the end of July, Willie?' McCadden prompted. 'Around the twenty-sixth.'

'The twenty-sixth? Of July? That was last month.'

'That's right.'

'Jaysus, I mean, the memory's not that good, you know—'

'The three of you were together then, weren't you?'

'I don't know, like I said, I—'

'You were, Willie. And something happened, didn't it?'

'Yeah?'

'Remind me what it was.'

'What it was?'

'Just like Rookie told it.'

'Rookie? How do you mean? What did Rookie say?'

'Upstairs? The vacant flat? The bit of bother?'

'Oh, that!' Flanagan squeaked. 'Yeah, that . . . I thought you meant . . . Yeah, well, we was sittin' in Rookie's kip. Just dossin', like. Playin' cards, you know. We heard this row upstairs. I didn't go up. Rookie an' Vinnie goes up. This American guy . . . We see in the papers he'd drowned. Logan . . . His name was Logan. Somethin' Logan . . . '

Flanagan was scared. So scared that the bits of the story he'd prepared wouldn't come out in the right sequence, wouldn't come together to make any real sense at all. He'd been sitting on it for almost four weeks now, living in terror of the moment someone was going to ask him about it. But not the police, McCadden thought. If he was frightened of cops, he would've shown it earlier, when McCadden and Smith arrived. Willie was scared of someone else.

McCadden considered him silently for a while. Then he asked, 'How much did Rookie Wallace give you, Willie, to spin that tale?'

Because McCadden knew now that Logan hadn't been in Dublin on 26 July. Logan had been in Waterford. Sonny Newburn would confirm it when he returned from holidays. But there were other proofs. Artie Logan, for instance, had taken nude photographs of Eleanor Shiels. Some of the shots had used the writing desk in the front room of her cottage as a prop. And on the desk, as McCadden had noted, there was a national newspaper, dated 26 July.

Flanagan didn't answer the question. He laughed a little hysterically, his mouth too dry and his brain too seized to get anything else out.

From behind McCadden, Chris Smith suddenly moved in. He leaned on the frail table, violently swept the rolled cigarettes off the surface, and pushed his face into Flanagan's. 'Wait a fucking minute!' he shouted threateningly.

Flanagan cringed and shrank backwards. 'What?'

'Hold the fucking horses, Willie!' Smith encouraged. 'July the twenty-sixth, you say?'

'What? What about it?'

'And three fellas, is it? All in balaclavas, maybe? One young guy, about medium height? One little runt of an older guy? And I'd say Rookie Wallace was a big man, with a strong build. Would I be right, Carl?'

McCadden nodded. 'That's him.'

'Fucking ace!' Smith celebrated. 'You weren't sitting around playing cards that day, Willie, were you?'

'We were! I was! I mean, I told you—'

'You'd just turned over the post office in Rialto, didn't you? With the help of a sawn-off shotgun and two iron bars. You and Vinnie Woods and Rookie Wallace. The three of you were dividing the fucking take!'

Smith pushed himself away from the table. He looked around. Deciding there were no respectable hiding places within reach, he disappeared into the bedroom, from where they could hear him noisily searching. When he came back, he was triumphantly flapping a wad of notes.

The odd thing was, when he counted it, the total was still almost a third of the amount taken in that robbery. Flanagan hadn't spent any of his cut. Hadn't risked being linked to it.

McCadden sat down on the opposite side of the table, with the banknotes spread across the surface between himself and Flanagan. 'You're not really worried about jail, are you, Willie?' he observed.

''Course I'm fuckin' worried . . . '

'No, you won't be going to jail, Willie. Not this time. Not if you help us out.'

'Wha'? You know I can't . . . '

'But maybe you don't want to help us out. Because you're worried about something else. And maybe you're right. The three of you saw something that day. You, Vinnie Woods and Rookie Wallace. Something dangerous. You know how I know that? Vinnie Woods's body was taken off a beach in County Waterford yesterday, Willie. He'd been filleted and thrown into the sea. And Rookie Wallace', McCadden lied, 'was shot the day before. The chances are, he's not going to pull through.'

McCadden paused, watching Flanagan's reaction. It was always possible that Wallace had returned to Dublin over the last twenty-four hours and made contact with Flanagan. But Flanagan had simply frozen, with his lips parted, ready to receive the cigarette his fingers were still holding in a crushing grip a couple of centimetres from his mouth.

'You got to help me,' he croaked then.

Smith was unsympathetic. 'You're on your own, Willie. Just like the other two.'

'Aren't you goin' to take me in?'

'Let's try a bit of novelty this time, Willie,' Smith suggested. 'First you talk to us, *then* we take you in.'

Flanagan started shaking. He tried to draw on the cigarette he'd finally slipped between his lips, but the fag had gone out. 'OK,' he said then. 'Yeah. OK, yeah. I mean, yeah, we was splittin' the take. Me, Vinnie, Rookie. Jaysus, I can't believe Vinnie . . . I just been talkin' to his mot. Yesterday. She never said nothin'.'

'She hasn't been notified yet, Willie. We're going over there now.'

'Fuck sake . . . '

'And the story?'

'Wha'?'

'What happened when you were splitting the take?'

'Yeah, well . . . There was this fuckin' thump from upstairs. I mean, we thought it was a fuckin' raid or somethin'. Vinnie, he was kinda high . . . So we went up, right? To check it out, like. I mean, this flat above Rookie's squat's supposed to be vacant an' all. The place was in darkness. We didn't bring no torch or anythin'. But after a while, you know the way your eyes . . . After a while we could see . . . There was this fella sittin on this chair inside. He looked dead. Beat up bad, anyways. But still moaning, like. And then this voice from behind him, from the dark . . . I mean, we couldn't see him or nothin'. This American voice. He says, walk away from it, guys. Just like that. You know? He was American. Walk away from it, guys, he says, it's nothin' got to do with you. And that's what we did. We got the fuck out of there.'

'Who was the dead man in the chair, Willie?' Smith asked.

'Wha'?'

'You didn't see the Yank. You walked away.'

'That's what I just told you.'

'But you're still scared of something. Who was the dead man?'

'You got to look after me here.'

'Who was the dead man, Willie? You recognized him, didn't you?'

'I need to know you're goin' to look after me.'

'Talk first, Willie, *then* we'll look after you.'

So Flanagan swallowed hard again and whispered, 'It was Tucker, wasn't it? Leo Tucker.'

Smith whistled. And slipped back into rhetorical style. 'Fuck me!' he invited.

twenty-five

Leo Tucker's body, tortured before he'd died and badly mutilated afterwards, had been found in the Dublin Mountains by a hill walker early on the morning of Saturday, 30 July, exactly three weeks earlier. He'd been buried in a shallow grave, which in turn had been concealed by cut bushes and fallen trees.

His murder was a drug-related gangland killing. That much was obvious. Tucker was a junior member of a Dublin family running cannabis and cocaine rackets in the capital. The news on the street, though, was that they were losing their grip. Others were muscling in on their trade. And a vicious turf war was in the air.

But no one knew who these others were. No one knew why Leo Tucker had been tortured and killed. And come to think of it, no one even knew where exactly he'd been murdered.

Willie Flanagan was the first witness to offer a significant lead in the case.

Chris Smith wanted to order a couple of reinforced police vans with protective wire meshing to lift Flanagan safely out of the estate, and was all for himself and McCadden hitching a ride back out with the convoy. McCadden was reluctant. He could see the virtue of getting Flanagan into custody before word spread that he was squealing to the cops, but he also wanted to interview Vinnie Woods's girlfriend and look at the squat Rookie Wallace had used.

'Look at it like this,' he invited Smith, after drawing him aside, out of Flanagan's hearing. 'The obvious explanation is that the guys who killed Tucker came after the three who witnessed it. But it doesn't stand up. Why track Woods to Waterford and leave Flanagan alone a couple of blocks from the scene? It makes no sense. Woods might have reason to go to ground. But he didn't go to Waterford to hide. He went there to follow Rookie Wallace. I've got to talk to Woods's girlfriend.'

But it wasn't an option. Not immediately, anyway.

'Vinnie's mot?' Flanagan said, when he was asked where she lived. 'She won't be there.'

'You said you talked to her yesterday.'

'Yeah, but she was on her way to her ma's. With the kid. Every Friday. She goes across to her ma's for the weekend, every Friday. With the kid.'

'Where does her mother live?'

'On the north side. Ballymun.'

McCadden jotted down the address and asked, 'What about Rookie Wallace's squat?'

'That's in the opposite tower. See there? You can see it from the window here. Number twenty-one.'

'You want to wait here, Chris?' McCadden asked Smith. 'I'll go and check it out.'

'Be careful,' Smith advised.

But that wasn't much of an option, either.

All the bulbs were smashed in the tower block opposite and the engineers seemed to have built the place with no regard for natural light. The grimy entrance hall reluctantly took in a little of the sunlight from the open doorway, but once McCadden turned the first corner the stairway ahead was black and spooky. He pressed his hand against the wall to steady himself, and jerked it quickly away again when it slithered in something soft and moist and indeterminate.

On the first-floor landing, a group of thin, hooded youths were huddled outside an open doorway, hiding from the light. They watched him suspiciously, knowing he was an outsider. It wasn't just that his face was unfamiliar. His clean clothes and obvious health offered too sharp a contrast to their grim poverty. He wondered how Rookie Wallace, with his height and strong build, had managed to pull it off, living as a squatter here. But he reckoned that Wallace's rough exterior and scarred face must've given the impression of a man on the run and too touchy to ask too many questions of.

On the darkened stairs, McCadden was wary of being followed and trapped, but he reached the third floor without anyone coming down against him or sneaking up behind him. By then his eyes had adapted to the dimness. Checking quickly along the landing, he saw that the door of number twenty-one was ajar. Boarded up by the local authority, it had been forced open again and then so badly abused that it was permanently warped and swinging freely.

Inside, in what was supposed to be the front room, there were three mattresses on the ground, all with heavy-duty sleeping bags on top. One lay across the doorway. Presumably it was wedged against the closed door at night to guard against intruders.

McCadden stepped carefully over it. From the kitchen beyond, he could hear the sound of voices arguing angrily. But not in English. And not in any European language he could recognize.

He crept forward and gently pushed at the kitchen door until it was open enough to offer a view.

Two men were standing at the sink with their backs to him. Both were short and stocky. Both were dressed in light jackets and dark blue jeans.

McCadden knocked hard and shouted, hoping that the more clumsy noise he made, and the more foolishly open he was, the less jittery the occupants might be. 'Excuse me!'

They turned sharply. But they also stayed close together all the time, never offering a glimpse of whatever they were preparing in the sink.

They looked Romanian, McCadden thought. And they were very, very tense. The guy on the right kept one hand behind his back, resting on the weapon he held there, concealed under the back flap of the jacket. And the quick glance he shared with the other asked only if he should use that weapon immediately or give it a little thought first.

These guys were dangerous, McCadden realized. Working off short fuses. Ignorant of the local scene. And probably desperate enough to use a gun as the first line of communication.

'Do you speak English?' he asked, in as level a voice as he could manage.

The one on the left jabbed a finger aggressively into his own chest. 'I speak English.'

'I'm looking for a man called Toomey,' McCadden improvised. 'His brother gave me this address. Number twenty-one.'

'Toomey?'

'You might know him as Socket,' McCadden suggested. 'His nickname. He's an electrician.'

The others looked puzzled. And the slow process of hearing in one language and mentally translating it into another gradually diluted their edginess. The one on the left frowned and testily shook his head. His friend said nothing, but kept his hidden weapon ready.

'No?' McCadden checked. 'I probably have the wrong block, have I? It must be twenty-one in one of the other towers. Thanks, anyway.'

He had to struggle to keep his movements under control as he left, backing casually out of the kitchen doorway, working through the mattresses sideways on, so that he never fully turned his back, and hurrying along the corridor once he got outside. He moved fast over the final stretch and was already turning on to the stairway before the pair reached the doorway of the squat in pursuit.

One of them called angrily. 'Hey! You wait!'

McCadden waved cheerfully and smiled benignly. *Difficulties with pronunciation*, his vague gesture apologized. Then he disappeared, sprinting down the stairs so fast that he was breathing hard by the time he reached the same hooded group on the first floor, who gave him the same suspicious examination while they were passing around the sodden butt of what looked like a limp reefer.

The sunlight at the tower block's entrance hit him hard, reminding him of his exit from the pub in Waterford a few days earlier. He didn't hang around to ease the adjustment this time. He blundered on. Through pinched eyes he had a blurred view of Chris Smith watching him from the window of Willie Flanagan's flat. He gave him a miniature signal, holding his right fist against his chest and jerking his thumb sideways, to indicate that they should go.

Smith read it accurately and met him at the entrance with Willie Flanagan. Flanagan's hands were still free. The sight of cuffs might've provoked a riot in the area.

With a small effort, the little man could've broken loose and made a run for it. But the news of Woods's death had drawn the fight out of him. He was scared. A station holding cell couldn't have been much of an attraction, but at least it was familiar. And safer than the streets.

With Flanagan shuffling along between them, the two detectives walked briskly out of St Anthony's Estate, back to the shopping district where they'd parked earlier.

Smith was relieved. McCadden wasn't so sure.

Settling into the back seat with Flanagan, he turned and leaned on the shelf, watching through the rear window. After the third corner, his suspicions were confirmed.

He said casually, 'We've picked up a tail, Chris.'

It was a dull, inconspicuous Toyota, sitting five or six spaces back. McCadden couldn't see its occupants. Its windscreen was either tinted or muddied.

'You sure?' Smith wondered.

'Take a left,' McCadden suggested.

Smith switched lanes and turned left, provoking a blast of car horns from irate drivers he'd cut across without warning. Behind them the Toyota quickly adjusted and performed the same manoeuvre, but more carefully, without drawing attention to itself.

'Yeah, I see it,' Smith confirmed. 'Hang on.'

He contacted the station on his radio, asked for back-up, and drove on afterwards at a relaxed pace, in straight lines, with all the appearance of leisurely knocking kilometres off a pre-arranged journey, until a squad car showed up in his rear-view mirror and settled into the line of traffic a little back from the Toyota. Smith took the first narrow side road then. He accelerated immediately, luring the Toyota into chasing him, and then braked suddenly, spinning the car sideways to block the width of the road.

The Toyota behind them, just starting to pick up speed, also braked hard. Realizing they'd been spotted, its driver tried to reverse out of the trap. But the squad car appeared at the road's entrance and cut off the escape.

Smith and McCadden sat it out. Through the side windows of their car, they watched a couple of uniformed officers cautiously approaching the stalled Toyota and stooping to talk to the driver and passenger. After a while, one of the uniforms straightened and walked – even more slowly it seemed – towards the detectives. He didn't look happy.

'Charlie,' Smith greeted him. 'What's the story?'

Charlie silently handed over a couple of wallets. Smith checked the contents of both. And swore. Without looking around, he passed the opened wallets back to McCadden. Each contained a Garda ID. One was for a Detective Sergeant Healy. The other was for a Detective Garda Crimmons.

'Why the hell are they following *us*?' Smith demanded.

Charlie knocked the peak of his cap upwards and scratched beneath the rim, as nonplussed as the next man. 'They didn't know who you were, sir, they say.'

'They picked us up at St Anthony's,' McCadden guessed. 'They must be on surveillance. Either Willie here, or Rookie Wallace's squat.'

Smith sighed. He looked out, past the uniformed guard, at a young woman behind the wheel of a silver Mercedes who was screaming at him to push the heap of shit he was driving off the middle of the road and let his betters through. Shaking his head, he twisted to face McCadden. 'This is going to take some sorting out,' he predicted. 'You know that? Some fucking sorting out.'

twenty-six

It took a whole day, a Minister for Justice, a Garda commissioner, two Chief Superintendents and a host of inspectors from Special Branch and the National Drugs Unit even to start the process of what Smith had called sorting it out.

They met on Sunday afternoon in a conference room at Garda Headquarters in the Phoenix Park. Outside the August heatwave was holding up through the weekend. The park was crowded with glowing young lovers and with tense families bickering in the sun. The nearby zoo was attracting lengthy queues and its most popular turn, as the papers reported the next day, seemed to be the small pond where the seals and penguins were cooling down and mocking their overheated observers.

In the dusty conference room, though, behind the closed curtains and the locked doors, the Minister for Justice, Niall McAwley, looked darkly irritated. He'd cancelled two photo opportunities to make this meeting, one with an Irish swimming champion who'd just given birth to healthy triplets, and the other with a group of refugees returning to their homeland in war-torn Kosovo. Sitting glumly at the head of the long oval table, he wore the expression of a man who knew he had better things to do, a man who hadn't entered politics to waste his Sunday afternoons avoiding self-promotion. He said nothing, letting the commissioner struggle with the burden of making the early running.

The commissioner wasn't in the best of shape, either. Appointed by the previous government and a public critic of zero tolerance – the Minister's fondest attention-grabbing gimmick – he wasn't in the humour to squeeze any joy from McAwley's discomfort. He was lost. Just as lost as the Minister. But unlike the politician he was feeling guilty about his failure and convinced that he was ultimately responsible for tidying the mess.

He had a scattering of notes in various hands spread across the surface of the table in front of him, and couldn't make sense of them, either individually or collectively. He'd just announced that someone had to start pulling this ragged story together and was now looking around the table for volunteers. But his men kept their heads down. Their eyes averted. Their brains wrestling with more vital matters. Pens. Paper clips. Punches. Just like schoolkids who dreaded being picked on to answer the teacher's most awkward questions.

Only McCadden, sitting at the centre of the long table, held the commissioner's look. A gesture the commissioner seemed to interpret more as an unacceptable challenge than an offer because he passed McCadden by and settled on a tall, thin superintendent further on.

'Roger?'

Roger Deanes was head of the National Drugs Unit. Loudly clearing his throat, he opened a bulging folder, took out a sheaf of documents and photographs, and handed them on to one of his inspectors to pass around.

He said, 'Some time ago, the Europol Drugs Unit, in The Hague, alerted us to the possibility that a ship named the *Kazra*, registered in St Vincent and carrying a large consignment of cocaine, intended landing the drugs here in Ireland, probably on an isolated south-coast beach, for later distribution in Ireland, England and mainland Europe. Europol already knew that the drugs belonged to a Colombian cartel. They did not know the identity of the importer here. Nor did we. But of course we were anxious to find out.

'The ship has been under close surveillance since the first alert. In the early hours of yesterday morning, the cocaine was unloaded at Breenlea Head, adjacent to Brownstown Head, in County Waterford. Two men previously unknown to us took delivery of the consignment on shore. From the copies of surveillance photographs handed out, some of you, however, will no doubt recognize them as Anthony Wallace, a serving member of the force, and Paul Hyland, a former detective sergeant stationed in Waterford.

'The movements of both have been closely monitored since. They travelled immediately to Dublin with the drugs. Early yesterday morning, Wallace went to a flat on St Anthony's Estate, which we believe he occupied as a squat, and made contact there with two Romanian nationals. We believe that the deal is scheduled to be concluded here, at this squat, perhaps this evening or tomorrow. Surveillance was therefore placed on the squat. When Inspector McCadden here visited it yesterday, he was not recognized by our officers and was consequently followed after leaving . . . '

McCadden had been studying the surveillance shots, taken in darkness with infra-red equipment. A tight, stony beach. In the background, the prow of the small boat that had been used to land there. Wallace and Hyland in the foreground. Tense and watchful. Armed. Sometimes holding sealed packages.

'What's the street value of the cocaine?' he asked.

'Impossible to tell until we've seized it, of course. But substantial. It's a major consignment. Twenty, thirty million pounds. The estimate is Europol's.'

'Where are Wallace and Hyland now?'

'At a Dublin address.'

The Minister sighed. He gravely mixed some metaphors that had bent cops carelessly staining the social fabric and then demanded to know who Wallace's superiors were. The focus shifted to Inspector Tom Reynolds. And Reynolds tried desperately to shift it on.

'For some time', he opened vaguely, 'Detective Garda Anthony Wallace has worked on a specific undercover operation in Dublin, supplying high-grade information on a major criminal gang with paramilitary links. His last recorded meeting with his handler was on Saturday, July the thirtieth. He seemed unusually tense and uncertain. He failed to keep his next appointment, on Friday, August the fourth. We had no knowledge of his whereabouts and feared for his safety. When a query about Wallace came from Inspector McCadden, originally on Friday, August the eleventh, we travelled to Waterford to check this out. Inspector McCadden was not co-operative, however . . . '

The Minister sighed again and chipped in with a popular campaign line about co-operation between state services being vital to efficiency.

McCadden only half-listened as Reynolds resumed afterwards. He was irritated by the man's evasiveness, his concern for nothing except enhancing or whitewashing his own role. And, besides, he had a little private analysis to complete before his own turn came to speak.

McCadden had a clearer idea now of what had happened over the last few weeks. If he'd been asked to talk first that afternoon, to open the session with his own account of events, he would've struggled badly, ignorant of the larger picture and still uncertain about the roles of others. But the news about the consignment of cocaine had put everything else in sharper perspective.

Back on the afternoon of 25 July, in the squat on St Anthony's Estate, Rookie Wallace, Vinnie Woods and Willie Flanagan, fresh from turning over a post office in an armed robbery, were nervously dividing the loot when they heard some weird noises from the vacant flat above them. Leo Tucker, caught trying to infiltrate a rival gang, was being tortured up there. When Wallace and Woods and Flanagan went up, they saw the unfortunate Tucker strapped to a chair and pleading for help. His captors were concealed in the shadows behind him.

On the grapevine – possibly as early as the next day – Wallace had discovered that the man behind the brutality was an Irish-American named Bill McMullan, who owned a pharmaceutical factory in Waterford. Like any good cop, Wallace had followed the lead.

It led him to Eleanor Shiels, on Brownstown Head in County Waterford.

Why? The only plausible explanation was that McMullan and Shiels were partners. And presumably lovers as well.

Not able to operate alone on separate fronts, Wallace had

asked McCadden to check out Eleanor Shiels for him while he returned to Dublin.

Like a good cop? Three days after holding up a post office in an armed robbery?

But the amazing thing was, that Wallace was still pretty straight back then. Or so McCadden believed. Wallace was still honest. He still intended exploding all this when the time was ripe. Until he got back to Dublin and finally discovered, from Leo Tucker's family, what all the fuss was about. Twenty million pounds worth of imported cocaine. And he found himself fancying a piece of it.

When McCadden imagined him making that act of betrayal . . .

It must've been at the end of a long corrosive process, of course, when Wallace was too disillusioned, too alienated to care any more, too successfully disguised as poor and on the make to remember anything different. A process that included the ill-conceived post-office robbery and probably some earlier lapses. A process that prompted Wallace to ask *McCadden* rather than the more up-to-speed Special Branch to check out Eleanor Shiels.

But when McCadden imagined the final decision, the moment when Wallace chose to go for it without the hope of ever returning, he thought of Wallace stranded in some isolated urban waste, waiting to make contact with his Special Branch handler and reading in the tabloids of the tacky tales of graft and corruption and fraud that his political masters wallowed in.

Wallace abandoned his operation in Dublin and came back to Waterford, probably around 1 August. Watching and waiting over the next few days, he discovered that Eleanor Shiels and Paul Hyland intended to double-cross McMullan. So he suggested an alliance, using the threat of a bust as a lever.

Or perhaps it was the other way round, McCadden accepted. Perhaps Wallace already knew Hyland as a former colleague. Perhaps it was *Wallace* who suggested the double-cross.

Either way, Wallace laid low and waited, thinking he was now in the clear. But he had two major problems.

Not the accidental death of Artie Logan.

McCadden didn't know whether Logan was in on the drugs deal or not. And he couldn't decide if the American's drowning was suicide or accident. But he knew it wasn't murder. Just as he knew that Logan was being pumped by Eleanor Shiels for information on McMullan's movements. And that Logan's death was an unwelcome but minor distraction for the plotters.

Wallace's problems lay elsewhere.

He was so absorbed by now, with his eyes fixed so steadily on the prize, that he'd forgotten about his request to McCadden.

When McCadden came back from holidays and turned up at Eleanor Shiels's cottage, Shiels alerted Wallace to the danger, probably after the funeral of Artie Logan the next day.

And that led to the second major problem.

Because Vinnie Woods, also fancying a piece of this rich cake, had followed the same trail as Wallace to Waterford. He sought out Eleanor Shiels, watched her cottage for a few nights and now tailed her to Wallace's hideout in the city.

Someone suggested meeting in the graveyard at Corbally crossroads. Possibly Woods himself. The kid was stupid. *Really* stupid. Flying high on amphetamines and crack, he'd spotted Cathy Morrison while waiting in the cemetery and tried to rape her. He was interrupted by Wallace. And killed.

One of Wallace's problems nicely down.

And one to go.

McCadden. Nosing closer and closer to disrupting the double-cross.

But between the three of them, Shiels and Wallace and Hyland, they knew exactly what would throw McCadden off the scent, knew exactly what script would paralyse him long enough for the deal to go down and the new millionaires to skip the country. The all too plausible tales of police corruption and political venality. Rookie Wallace as the hunted hero. Eleanor Shiels as the old-time political radical, reinvigorated for one more fight against a rotten establishment.

And – it must have finally occurred to one of them – why not actually *use* the enthralled McCadden instead of just keeping him in captivity? Because Bill McMullan needed to be shifted off the scene as well.

Still sexually entangled with Eleanor Shiels, McMullan had been set up the night the drug shipment was landed at Breenlea Head. Lured to Eleanor Shiels's cottage, from where he must have intended slipping away to Breenlea Head in the early hours, he'd been drugged and abandoned, left sprawling in the midst of scattered blood, to be discovered and arrested after Hyland's call had alerted McCadden.

As a scheme it was beautifully crafted, McCadden had to admit. Beautifully improvised. Ingenious. Almost perfect.

But looking again at the surveillance photos of Wallace and Hyland bringing in the cocaine that night, he felt only a deep sadness. There was something unbearably tragic about their predicament, he thought. Something that suggested the point-lessness of human endeavour, the role of men as blind puppets. All that intelligence, all that creativity and all that superb reading and manipulation of character, and all the time the enterprise was doomed to failure. While the three dreamed and plotted, daring to imagine success, the men from the drug squad, like minor malevolent gods, lurked unseen in the darkness, steering everything towards ruin.

McCadden didn't tell the full story, or what he knew of the full story, when his turn came at the conference table that afternoon. He buried his own role in concealing Rookie Wallace. And he said nothing at all about Bill McMullan.

These things were for later. In a private interview with the commissioner. Who wouldn't hang him out to dry. He hoped.

For the moment . . .

Rookie Wallace had come to Waterford to cut himself in on a major drugs deal organized by Eleanor Shiels and Paul Hyland for an unknown bankroller. He made the mistake of unwittingly involving McCadden, who followed his nose and found himself in Dublin . . .

It was as simple as that.

twenty-seven

McCadden was thrown the role of observer in the big sting. A dry bone to distract an old dog.

He didn't mind. For the most part, he'd already lost interest in the case. Another drugs story, he thought gloomily. Another noisy bust, with or without gunfire.

It was a cliché.

In itself, McCadden felt, the importation of drugs was about as fascinating as the importation of car parts. People did it for profit. The mystique was added later by those, from both sides of the fence, who had an interest in hyping the scene. Dealers and users, police and politicians. Scruffy cops with Uzi sub-machine guns and flashy gang bosses with gold-plated pistols. Self-important nonentities. Bit players in a tedious melodrama.

And a melodrama in which McCadden no longer had an active role.

He'd made his private report to the commissioner. The commissioner had raised an eyebrow once or twice. Not at McCadden's failure to turn in Rookie Wallace. There was nothing officially against Wallace at the time. And the fault lay with Special Branch. The surprise was prompted by McCadden's eagerness to believe in the total corruption of an important section of the force.

It told against him, McCadden saw. And it would still tell against him when the time came to make the next round of promotional appointments. There was no room for sceptics at the top table. Only the faithful could expect to inherit.

The commissioner's frown of disapproval was balanced some-what by a pat on the back for uncovering McMullan. It was secretive praise, though. There would be no public move against McMullan, who'd left the country on a flight for Boston shortly after being discharged from the hospital in Waterford. On the basis that it was impossible to get a politician to keep his mouth shut, the commissioner accepted that the American must've been alerted to the danger he was in by the babbling Minister for Justice.

McMullan could run. But he wouldn't last long. If the FBI didn't quickly find him after a tip-off from their Irish counter-parts, then his disappointed business partners would exact bloody revenge for losing the shipment of cocaine.

On a slightly smaller scale, McMullan's disappearance would ultimately lead to the closure of the pharmaceutical factory in County Waterford. It was possible that some of the profits from the drug deal had been earmarked to consolidate Lisenter. It was also possible, of course, that the pharmaceutical plant was intended as a cover for illegal operations and for laundering its profits. But the collapse of the factory would have a devastating effect on the economy of the region, leading to widescale redundancies and long-term unemployment and plunging some of the local families back into poverty.

McCadden's inability to shake off a niggling sense of respons-ibility for the coming disaster was at the source of his gloomy mood and his reluctance to stay involved. There were no real successes in investigative police work, he decided. The damage had already been done. Murder. Theft. Destruction. Whatever it was, all you ever did was uncover it.

But the commissioner was insistent. 'You've brought it this far,' he encouraged, 'you might as well see it through.'

So McCadden saw it through. But with the enthusiasm of a man condemned to watching a dire soap opera on TV.

Stuck with two young drug-squad officers whose taste in music made him aware of his advancing age, he sat in an unfurnished vacant flat on one of the older estates close to St Anthony's with a clear view of Rookie Wallace's squat.

It was supposed to be a straightforward operation.

The leading members of the Tucker family had already been lifted in case they fouled things up by trying to muscle in or exact revenge for the dead Leo. And Bill McMullan was no longer in the picture. Which left only the Romanians as buyers and Wallace and Hyland and Eleanor Shiels as sellers.

The coke was stashed in a white touring van, parked outside a guest house in the prosperous southern suburbs where the three were staying. It was expected that the van would be driven to St Anthony's and the deal cut there.

But someone had written the wrong script.

Over the radio McCadden listened to the reports from the officers watching the white touring van as it pulled away on its journey. Paul Hyland and Eleanor Shiels were posing as a couple. Hyland was driving. Shiels was in the front passenger seat. No one seemed really certain where Rookie Wallace had placed himself. The consensus favoured the back of the van.

The reports from the checkpoints along the route were dull at first. Routine. Relaxed.

The calm was replaced by a slight surprise, though, when the van unexpectedly took a right turn instead of holding to the main carriageway. The surprise was dislodged by worry as it continued on this new course without correcting itself. And near panic set in when everyone finally realized that its destination was actually the car-ferry terminal at Dun Laoghaire.

They weren't going to cut a deal at St Anthony's at all. They were going to bring the cocaine to England.

As the van joined the short queue for the ferry, the head of the drugs-squad, monitoring the operation from his command post, eventually made his call. Move in, he ordered. Take the van, its contents and its occupants.

It was quickly over. A non-event. The surrounding units closed in. For a minute or two, the traffic on the radio seemed like the sound-track of a bad cop drama on TV. The public was momentarily alarmed . . .

And while the bust was still in progress, a battered Renault Mégane rolled into St Anthony's Estate and pulled up outside the block where Rookie Wallace had his squat.

McCadden smiled to himself as he watched Wallace stepping

out of the car, carrying a heavy-duty shopping bag. Unable to stretch their trust in each other, the three conspirators had obviously split the haul of coke. Hyland and Shiels had their own thing going. Wallace was doing a private deal with the Romanians.

Watching him being swallowed up by the dark entrance to the tower block, the two drug-squad officers started to get anxious. Their mobile back-up units, already drawn to the action at the ferry terminal, were now a couple of kilometres away, skidding frantically into U-turns to get back again in response to the call. But things moved fast. Too fast.

Within minutes of Wallace's appearance, the two Romanians were leaving the tower block, carrying that same heavy-duty shopping bag. When they also got into Wallace's car, fired the engine and noisily pulled away, there was only one possible call. The drug-squad officers would have to track them, directing the returning units to intercept. And McCadden would toss a coin when they were gone. Either hold the fort, waiting for back-up, and lose Wallace if he didn't also stay put. Or move in for a quick collar. And lose Wallace anyway, if he resisted decisively enough.

All the signs, though, suggested that Wallace intended cutting out immediately. Through the windows of the squat, using the powerful binoculars set up for the surveillance, McCadden caught glimpses of him collecting personal items, presumably for a hurried packing. One of these seemed to be a second set of keys. Perhaps for another of the cars that were parked below, where he'd pulled up earlier in the Renault.

McCadden left the observation post. He crossed the footbridge over the canal between the two estates, entered St Anthony's through a gap in the steel fencing and took the same route as the previous day into the darkness of the tower block. Up the grimy stairway. Along the dank corridor. Into the front room, where the three narrow mattresses still lay together.

Ironically, Wallace was in the same position as the Romanians had been the day before, washing his hands at the sink in the kitchen. On the floor by his feet lay the holdall he'd just packed.

McCadden knocked on the kitchen door.

For a moment, as Wallace swivelled in response to the noise, his right hand tugging at the butt of the automatic weapon wedged in his belt, McCadden worried that he was going to be shot. But the gamble paid off. Wallace was too surprised to actually carry the movement through. He started thinking, wondering how the hell *McCadden* had arrived in front of him, and the process dulled his instincts. The gun stayed inside his belt.

McCadden kept his hands in the open, raised in front of his chest, eager to demonstrate that he had no weapon of his own. 'You keep forgetting about me,' he said.

Wallace stared at him intently. 'Are you alone?' he asked.

'No,' McCadden bluffed. 'I asked to come in and talk to you first.'

'Why?'

McCadden shrugged. The gesture was as much a release of tension as a partial answer. He knew now that the immediate danger was past. But to build on it he had to find an engaging line of dialogue to string Wallace along and keep him talking until the back-up arrived.

It wasn't difficult.

'Did you really listen to a recording of "Crazy Man Michael" the last time you saw your parents?' he wondered.

Wallace frowned. 'You came up here to ask me that?'

'It's part of a larger question.'

'What?'

'How much of the truth were you telling me when you called at my flat in Waterford the other day? About your own past?'

'What difference does it make?'

'You made a mistake, sharing the same memory with Eleanor Shiels as well as with me. She sang "Crazy Man Michael" in the local pub on Friday night.'

Wallace shrugged. 'It's a good song.'

'Too much of a coincidence.'

'Maybe it's becoming more popular.'

'The past always betrays us.'

Wallace laughed. 'I know what betrayed me. It wasn't my own past.'

McCadden heard footsteps on the stairway and in the corridor outside the squat. The pace of their movement told him that it was armed drug-squad officers. There was something else he wanted to say before they reached him, something about 'Crazy Man Michael', about Wallace's sense of betrayal by the state he'd served for eighteen years, but he couldn't get it together in time.

He watched the drug-squad officers filtering past him on either side as they came through the kitchen doorway, their weapons raised and pointing at Wallace. He watched Wallace weighing the odds against him, abandoning any lingering hope of escape and then considering whether it was better to die quickly now or die slowly as an ex-cop in prison.

When Wallace drew the gun from his belt, it was, McCadden felt, merely an empty gesture, inviting execution. Wallace knew that he had no chance of victory, and little of survival, if he threatened.

Amid the noisy chaos afterwards, amid the shouted instructions and curses and warnings, one of the drug-squad officers, probably scared that he was first in the line of Wallace's fire, panicked a little earlier than was necessary. He squeezed the trigger of the revolver he was holding.

McCadden ducked when he heard the gunshot, knowing that it was going to provoke others in such a tense situation. He was still too late. He saw Wallace recoiling and crumbling. He felt a sharp blow to his own left shoulder. And then he lost consciousness . . .

twenty-eight

It was only in hospital, when he had too much free time while recovering from the gunshot wound to his shoulder and nothing much to do with it except think, that McCadden finally captured what he'd wanted to say to Rookie Wallace.

His visitors were numerous enough and attentive enough to keep him from brooding during the day. The death of Rookie Wallace in the shoot-out at St Anthony's, they all reckoned, the loss of an acquaintance in such circumstances, was a traumatic event to witness. And the arrest of another friend and former colleague, Paul Hyland, wasn't going to help the healing process. So they rallied to his bedside.

But ironically, it was the visitors themselves who jogged McCadden's memory. Their character. Their motives.

He had no personal callers.

He had a humorous get-well card from Cathy Morrison, posted in Los Angeles, blaming him for the demise of the Irish film industry. Apparently, the production of *Sacrifice* had folded during the fourth week of location shooting. Its cast and crew unpaid. Its major financial backer, Bill McMullan, bankrupt and disappeared. Yet another casualty of the seized cocaine shipment.

He had a typically unsympathetic note from Roberta Gavin, regretting not seeing him during her recent visit to Waterford, but pointing out that he was to blame for the loss.

His ex-wife was on holiday in Japan, where her new husband seemed to be studying garden design.

And that was it.

The rest of his visits were all professional.

Counsellors came and went. The young drug-squad officer whose ricochet had done for McCadden's shoulder turned up to apologize. Frank Ryan drove a group of colleagues up from Waterford and brought with him a wide selection of confectionery, half of which he ate himself. And most significantly of all, on the day after the surgeons took the bullet from McCadden's shoulder, the commissioner showed, left his entourage outside the door of the room and sat in private with McCadden, assuring him of a central role in the new Murder Squad, whether or not he recovered in time to present himself to the interview board.

McCadden thanked him. But he knew now that the top job was beyond him. The head of the new Murder Squad would be a more circumspect appointment, representing less risk than McCadden carried with him. A competent functionary. A man who would use McCadden's talents, while filtering out his awkwardness.

It was, after all, a political position. Now that the Minister for Justice, Niall McAwley, had been weakened by the fallout from the McMullan coke deal, the commissioner would strengthen his own position by planting a trusted lackey in the vacant seat, protecting his flank and tilting the balance of power back in his own favour. Ability had nothing to do with it. Connections were everything.

It was a gloomy thought.

And as he lay alone in darkness in the hospital ward that night, with only the dry cough of a nearby patient and the clack of a nurse's shoes on the bare tiles to disturb his concentration, McCadden dwelt on it.

There was so little difference between himself and Rookie Wallace, it occurred to him. Two lives defined by dedication. But not dedicated to anything in particular. Not to a cause or a party, for instance. Not to a church or an ethic. Just dedication for the sake of absorption. Hanging on to the respectable side of the law by the thin threads of remembered values from their own childhoods, their upbringing in a different era. And if the threads snapped, as they had with Wallace, neither had anything of substance to fall back on. No faith, as Wallace had pointed out. No religion. No system of values. No family. No tradition. Two floating men, trying to lever the world without a foothold of their own.

The similarities – the shock of having his own image reflected and distorted at the same time – probably explained McCadden's dogged, uncertain pursuit of Wallace. He was, literally, chasing his own shadow. It also probably explained his reluctance to turn Wallace in, his willingness to believe in the possibility of a hero.

And since he was lying in a hospital bed when the comparison came to him, surrounded by illness and death, it also scared him a little.

Perhaps Wallace's more ambitious reach, his deeper idealism, his own exalted notions of service and sacrifice, had all betrayed him in the end. Perhaps McCadden's more modest scale, his tendency to prefer the local to the national picture, his preference for the individual over the group, marked the saving difference between them. He liked to imagine, for instance, that he wouldn't have fallen for the sorcerer's trick of confusing corrupt politicians with an entire society and lashing out at both without distinction.

Perhaps.

But McCadden also found it sad, thinking of Wallace's wasted intensity and passion, thinking of Eleanor Shiels's banal decline from self-destructive but honest rebel in the early seventies to commercial opportunist at the turn of the millennium.

All that withered idealism from a more naive age . . .

The cliché'd journey that all his generation had taken . . .